I0587019

THE WATER WORDS

Jessica Hecket

The Water Words
Copyright © 2012, 2018 Jessica Hecket

All rights reserved. No part of this book may be reproduced in any form without permission in writing from the author, except in the case of brief quotations embodied in critical articles or reviews.

This is a work of fiction. Names, characters, places, events, and incidents are either the product of the author's imagination or used in a fictitious manner. Any resemblance to actual persons, living or dead, or actual events is purely coincidental.

ISBN-13:978-0-9994364-3-1

2 3 4 5 6 7 8 9 10

Cover Design by Leslie Connly
Title Layout by Rachael Ritchey

*For my Father, My Counselor, and my Friend, who lets
me know I am never alone.*

And for Mom and Dad, who introduced me to Him.

Water runs, water falls.
Water rises, water calls.

Water crashes, water breaks.
Water freezes, water takes.

Water gives, water flows.
Water speaks, water knows

I

Aylia stood on the dock hugging a piling as she looked out at the Sea. Her hazel eyes absorbing the brilliant colors as the sun slowly sank behind the glowing Veil. She wondered what the sun could now see from its vantage. There was something, something wonderful across the Sea, behind that distant bank of fog that shrouded her view of the horizon. Bright pink and strong orange transformed the misty wall for a short time as the sun fizzled behind it with a soft golden light. The celestial warmth caused small streams of white vapor to escape from the Veil and move toward her.

Sighing she hopped off the dock and the sea giggled as it splashed around her ankles. Gently lapping around her legs, ripples spoke in a multitude of tiny chime like voices, "*come play, come play, we play along the beach today.*" Smiling down at the water she watched as it amusingly distorted her reflection. Then, sweeping her foot through the shallow surf, she listened as the little voices rose in laughter like children being spun on a carousel. Ripples were always playful at sunset. Moving softly over the water, the wind touched her face and blew sandy blonde strands of hair out of her eyes as she gazed at the colorful horizon once more.

The words of the water were comforting. This evening the voice of the surf was joyful and gentle. Walking along the beach she listened to the Sea. Few among the Sea Folk listened to the water anymore. Aylia found an unexplainable delight in the hearing of the languid speech within the shallows. She never felt alone upon the shore. Her eyes were moved to the great waves. Rolling and crashing, bellowing roars that shook her very being. She stood up a little straighter, inspired by their courage as they moved like an army attempting to conquer the land. The turbulence of the waves reminded her that the Sea is a dangerous place. The massive Ocean of her world stood as a barrier, separating two very different lands.

Beyond the memory of mankind, the Sea rests on its foundations as a great divide, separating the mortal from the immortal. Full of wisdom and light the ethereal continent is home to beautiful and fearsome creatures; beings that have now passed from legend to myths. Now, upon the mortal shore, only one small oddity of a nation, Arcadia: home of the Sea Folk, dares to remember. Most of the human race, dare not to venture out upon the sea for fear of those that dwell beneath the waves. Aylia was born among the Sea Folk during the time when the Light put a plan into motion that would one day unite the two shores. Messengers from the forbidden land were sent. Not bound by a permanent state of flesh they overcome the Sea by passing into spirit, bringing visions and dreams in small glowing spheres to a chosen few at first. They sought to awaken those destined to shine in the heavenly lights. For Aylia the dreams had come first. Over and over again dreams of finding treasure in pools of water. It was a vibrant dream, full of color. *Squatting on her knees, digging in shallow pools along the shore, and finding gold coins in wet sand. She fumbled through them with her fingers, tingling with a strange sensation between joy and disbelief. On the front of each coin was a face, she couldn't quite make out, but her heart leapt and she knew this was gold from across the Sea. It was the King's gold. Such treasure was beyond measuring. When she moved to jump up and run to her family, her mother suddenly appeared, throwing the gold back into the pond and telling her,*

"You don't know what you're messing with, Child! Leave it alone!" Aylia fought and tried to find her voice, but soldiers on horseback appeared and took her away. The dream had troubled her at first; it nagged at her heart and mind constantly, like a pebble in her shoe. It kept reoccurring, each time more intense than the one before. Sometimes she burst out of sleep as the guards took her away.

Searching for answers she had begun to spend time alone at the shore watching the water; longing to understand the vision. A few times she had even dug into the sand, wondering if it could be possible that a gold coin might be found there. And she searched for a treasure from the other shore; she began to hear the water words. As the water slapped against the side of a boat or pier she heard, *"get back, get back."* As waves objected to man-made intrusions which hindered their waltz with the wind. Rolling swells called out in fun, *"whoooaaa, whoooaa, here we goooo!"* as they rose and fell. Yet, it was in the shallows that she heard the most. The words were softer, but in stillness the water was more inclined to speak of memories than motion. The Sea was full of memory, memories of the distant shore. Today it was speaking about *him* again; the one who had given it voice and song. She smiled as the many little voices filled her head.

Aylia was puzzled, however, when the water posed a question. *"Have you seen him, have you seen him? He is here, he is here."* She stood still and turned toward the water and bent down. She had always spoken back to the Water as freely as it spoke to her. "Who is here?" Her voice seemed so young and hollow as it floated above the ageless element of the water. The sea swirled around her feet as the surf continuously moved upon the sand. It trembled around her as it spoke, *"He is here, HE is here…...he comes, he goes, he ebbs, he flows."*

Aylia stood up and slowly swayed as she strolled along the beach. She watched her feet sink into the submerged sand as she walked. It took balance to walk in the surf. The water pushed you toward the land, and then tried to pull the sand out from under your feet. Aylia was now deft at walking where the land and sea met.

He comes, he goes, he ebbs, he flows. He *ebbs*, he *flows*? Over and over again the words swirled through her mind like the wavelets that had spoken them. Her gaze strayed again to the horizon. She had heard a few old tales that hinted about the mysteries behind the Veil. Yet, she knew little about then, only boys were sent to the temples to learn the laws, and those gave little information about things that remained unseen. The Sea Folk or Waterbearers were a conquered people. The foreigners from the North who had overtaken the Sea Folk did not hope for a new Shore, but sought to control the present one. Aylia turned around and meandered her way back to the dock. Her lack of knowledge frustrated her. As she climbed up onto the wooden landing she wondered if her father might take them to Navar. It was the nearest city. There she could seek out a Talebearer with her questions. Yet, the thought gave her no comfort as she looked longingly across the waves, for she realized her answers lay beyond the Veil that now hid them from her view.

A small boat was visible now as it approached. Closing her eyes she turned back and took a deep breath, the clean salty air filling her nose and clearing her head. Opening her eyes it seemed as if the Veil was parted and she saw bright light dancing unbridled upon the water, and what appeared like a city of gold shone as the sun across the waves. She shivered as a cool gust of wind affronted her and the vision faded. Evening was coming and she hugged herself as she wondered about someone across the sea. Something deep inside her knew he was there, and more than that, he knew she was listening.

The heavy footsteps of her father on the wooden planks called her attention and she looked up to see him looking at her. "Hello, lovely!" He reached out and took her by the hand and pulled her up into a bear hug. She couldn't help but be happy in his presence. Tabor was a good man, strong and solid in spirit, dressed in traditional fisherman gear, and wearing a great smile. Looped across his shoulders was a rope he was working on and in his hand was a string of today's catch. He was sweaty, tired and happy. Walking arm in arm down the dock he began to tease her. "Well, now," he began as he looked at her out of the corner of his sharp eye, "How early were you able to get out of you chores today, so you could feint waiting for your old man as you listened to the sea?" She looked up at him anxiously. But before she could protest to his question he laughed heartily. Jostling her a bit he told her not to worry. "I know you love being here to see me home, but I am not ignorant about how you spend your time." Her gaze fell as he continued. "I listen now, but I have yet to understand the words." He looked down with pride upon his daughter and his voice became soft, "It is a special gift you have, my dear." As they left the shore and moved onto the street they were lost in their own thoughts. Aylia had become careful when speaking about the water words. Learning to be reserved had been a painful habit she had adapted over the past year or so. Mixed responses from friends and relatives had caused painful misunderstandings and so they had taught her to be selective about what she shared.

The dust from the road puffed around their feet with each step. Twilight had come and the street was empty of people. Aylia spoke softly, "Daddy, may I ask you something?" He looked down at her and said, "Anything." He watched her face. Although she was small for her age, her time on the shore *listening* had caused her to develop deeper understanding and an

6

inner peace that was not common for one of only twelve years. "What do you know of the king who is said to have lived across the sea?" Tabor was not surprised by the question, but he was unsure how to answer it. He looked up at the sky thoughtfully, searching for words. "I don't know. I do know there once was such a king. And that he gave great favor to our people and was our king for a time, under his rule we were a great nation, but the Tales say that he left and went back to his home across the sea long ago."

Aylia was eager for more, "So, this King, he is the one who will set us free?" Tabor lowered his voice now and looked around as they kept moving. They were nearly home and it was dark out. Lamps were being lit in houses as families prepared for dinner. Tabor answered thoughtfully, "Well, I know many believe the Promise he spoke of will be a great High King. Many are hoping he will arise soon and free us from the Sackeens." Aylia replied with open curiosity, "So do you believe the Promise will be a warrior who will lead us in a revolt?" His brow furrowed, of course this was what everyone hoped for, every time they were over taxed or mistreated by the soldiers. Sackeens killed openly anyone who protested, even those who simply could not meet their demands. Their society was superior in their eyes and they had no sympathy or understanding for the simple Waterbearers they had conquered. A Seaman would be a liar to say he did not wish to see the Sackeens driven from the Shore country by the violence of vengeance. His answer to her now did not stem from great knowledge, but rather from a wisdom he himself did not know the origin of, "The Promise will come from the King himself, and will more than likely be a riddle to men, as the King is. I cannot allow myself to think that I have enough understanding to know what the Promise will, or will not be. A king for sure, but not like the king we are now under I am certain, and so I have nothing to compare him to, except the very worst example." These reflections filled Aylia and triggered something deep within her. She sighed softly. "I think the Water was speaking of him today." Tabor looked down at her with great interest. He planned to ponder her statements that night, as they were now close to home. "Father, I was wondering if we could…" but she never finished her question. She stopped in mid-sentence because standing in front of their house and was a Sackeen guard.

They both startled at his presence and Tabor struggled to give him a proper greeting as his mind raced, searching for a reason for a soldier to be at his home. He tightened his grip around Aylia's shoulders protectively. The foot soldier only stepped aside and swung the door open, revealing an orange glow from within. He waved his spear for them to enter. As Aylia stepped inside, she saw her mother rise from her chair at the sight of her only to be slammed back into it. Rapha's beautiful face was streaked with tears and Tabor entered with the outer guard on his heels. The house was little more than a thatched hut and the presence of three soldiers made the atmosphere feel thick and close. The Captain rose from a chair and observed Aylia. The other soldier grabbed her by the shoulders and pushed her toward his commander. Tabor stepped up beside her and received the sharp point of a spear under his chin to keep him back. The eyes of the soldiers were curious and wary of the young girl they were here for. She looked back at the Captain with big eyes. "How old are you girl?" She tried to speak but her peace seemed gone from her. She stammered as she answered, "nearly thirteen summers, my lord." She looked to her mother again. The Captain took her chin and made her look into his face once more. "You don't appear to be anything out of the ordinary, but never mind, the

Searchers call for you." Tabor looked to his wife and her eyes confirmed what he feared. The soldiers were marking Sea Folk children for sacrifice.

Tabor cried out in protest as Aylia was taken outside. A swift hit to his gut with the broad end of the spear caused him to double over. Rapha went to his side, and a soldier positioned himself over them to keep them from interfering. Aylia was led away from the house to where more soldiers were waiting near the road with a small fire. She was pushed to her knees and her hair was yanked up, causing her to lift her head and expose her neck. Two guards held her fast. One of the men walked toward her with a small hot iron from the fire. He looked at her and paused for just a moment, curious that she wasn't crying out. Water flowed from her eyes in small steady streams. She could hear the moan of each tear as it rolled down her cheek. Their cries matched those of her heart. She searched for the faces of the men in the darkness, trying to make out their features in the orange light. A single cry drowned out those of her tears as the hot iron was pressed against the side of her neck. The mark was small, the emblem strange. Smoke rose from the wound and singed her nostrils.

She was brought back into the house and handed over to her mother. The Captain looked to Tabor now, "You know the penalty if she cannot be found?" Tabor rose with a gaze that threatened to melt the soldier's armor. The Captain extended his staff and lifted Tabor's chin with the sharp blade, "I asked you a question, Seaman!" Blood dripped down the end of the spear as Tabor replied. The soldiers turned to leave. When they were gone Tabor slumped over the table and wept aloud. Every bit of his being cried out for help. The wind was blowing strong tonight and he hoped it would carry his cries to the mysteries of hope that lay beyond the Veil.

Unnoticed on the rooftop, Lightscab perched, watching closely all that transpired. A creature from the other shore, he had a striking appearance, but his presence gave off a soft golden light that soothed. If person could perceive him, his appearance would be like a large eagle-like man. His wings flashed white and quivered as flames. As Tabor's cry rose into the night sky, the Lightscab took to the air. The wind was not dependable enough to carry such an earnest charge across the turbulent Sea. As he glided over the weakening sound, he opened his wings wide before lowering them in a swift beat. He worked deftly yet carefully to nestle the words into the hollows under his wings. Then, turning quickly he headed toward the Veil. In what appeared to be no more that the twinkle of a distant star, he was gone.

Darkness lurks
And darkness waits.
To grasp and hold
To share its fate.

Watching, keeping,
Poised to strike.
Forever banished
From the Light.

Rage, and Malice
Toil and Strife
Set to confuse
Our Way in life.

Light can break
Their monstrous hold
Sleeping warriors
Arise, be Bold!

2

Looking down over the shores of men, a large pair of eyes danced at the scene before them. From his perch on the northern border sat the hunched form of Malice. The cries of Sea Folk filled the night. The dark figure strained to catch every moan. Tonight he was a composer reveling in the triumph of his symphony of anguish. A grumble of laughter rose in his throat. His eyes were squinted against the pale light of the moon that fell through the sky and bounced on the waves.

His solitary delight was shortly interrupted by one of his minions. A strong spirit, named Bain, came up like a whirlwind toward his lord. Malice tumbled off his perch and scrambled behind it at Bain's presence. Malice let out an angry cry. Bain's appearance was pathetic. He was diminished in a withered state of illumination. He quickly crouched behind a rock. In the shadow he felt some relief. Even the dim moonlight had aggravated his wounds. He had two large gashes where he had actually been struck by a ray of First light. Unhindered this light causes damage to Shadows and Leeches, and in great volume will even make Furies flee. Although Bain's wounds were minor, he was completely inflamed with white light. Even the eyes of a mortal could have perceived him as he had reduced to a more fleshly state in order to recuperate. He leaned against the large stone. It was just as well to be far from Malice as he gave his report. Malice demanded answers for his condition. "What happened?" His voice sounded like a low hiss. "Don't tell me branding a few fishermen's daughters was too great a task for one such as Bain." Bain sneered at the remark but answered quickly, "I did all that was in my power. We were heavily outnumbered." His excuse was weak and he knew it. Malice questioned him, "Lightbearers? Lightbearers interfered with the marking of the young?" Bain thought back with some effort. "No, my lord, our task is done." Malice grew impatient, "Then what happened, you idiot?!" Bain gasped as he spoke, "One of the girls was particularly violent in her struggle. She injured one of the soldiers and..." Malice had grown tired of Bain's strained voice, braving the sting of the light; he leapt over the boulder and pounced on him. Digging his claws in deep, Malice held Bain up and eyed the Shadow carefully. From the looks of things, Malice concluded that it must have been some sort of ambush. But even then, wouldn't Bain have tried to retreat? His wounds were small, but the illumination was the mystery, it appeared as if Bain had remained in an area of light for an extended period of time, without a covering of man flesh to sustain him. Bain was too weak to show fear as he sobbed wretchedly in Malice's grip. "Bain," Malice shook him to attention, he spoke softly unleashing a strong persuasive strain into his speech "Bain, why did you not flee?" Bain lifted his head and looked at Malice as if under a trance "He...*He*...required respect." His moans and cries became pitiful. Malice looked around anxiously trying to understand how such a strong Fury could be so reduced in a brief encounter. "What do you mean, *He?*" He cringed at the pain caused by his touching one so drenched in light. But he bore it and demanded Bain to make more sense. Bain choked on the words. Malice interrogated him for hours. It was only by putting together the rambled bits of gargled narration that he came to have a vague understanding of what had occurred.

Light will come in the darkest night.
As a heart, receives its Sight.

3

In the southern part of the Shore country, a Seaman named Samuel and his family had been asleep when the soldiers visited them. Samuel and his wife were held down in their bed while their eighteen-year-old daughter Oya was ripped out of her blankets. She fought violently against the men as they overpowered her. In her desperation something was birthed within. Strange, wonderful, and powerful a holy *wrath* ignited. Heat began to burn within her chest. Like a seed in the earth, which may lay dormant for years and then suddenly sprout when the rain comes, Oya's gift burst forth ferociously in her hour of need. She received *Vision*, the eyes of her heart opened to the fiery spirit world. She could *See* not only the dark figures of the soldiers, but the strange forms of spirits that were present among them. Something akin to fire, small at first, a mere spark, trembled in her heart and a dull glow shone up her neck and shoulders. It was not as though the flame was being kindled, but as if *glow* was being born. Though unseen by the others present, its effects were felt. The Sackeen officers could not understand why, but they became afraid of her. Wrestling her outdoors they looked to their commander for confidence. The struggle ceased as she let out a cry, a great unintelligible mingling of frustration and release, as her spirit ignited. An orange red glow began to emanate from her chest. As if her heart was a flame and her body a lamp shade. Her skin seemed almost transparent as the glow spread throughout her body. The Light of the Far shore shone within her. Oya became the union of the Light and mortal flesh, as Glory burned, empowering her spirit and quickening her body rather than destroying it. One soldier had her by the arm. Another by her legs as they drug her from the house without perceiving the Light. All the while she was aware that a power or presence was being released through her in orange and yellow hues. Although the soldiers were blind to what was happening to her, the hair on their bodies prickled on end and they grew uneasy. In this moment Oya turned and bit down hard on the hand that held her wrist. The soldier screamed out in pain and annoyance as he released her. With her hand free, and to her own amazement, she reached up and took hold of the other soldier's armor and bracing her feet against his belly and in one quick movement flung him over the top of her and into the other officer.

Oya stood to her feet now completely aglow. Her hands felt hot and she brushed them together and watched as light sparked from her palms. She tried again and the sparks grew larger. She could hear words she did not understand and realized that the strange speech was coming from her mouth. The men looked at one another in disbelief. A few of them began to consider that perhaps she was possessed by a demon. She was working in a state beyond impulse or instinct; she was a vessel, giving shape and flavor to the glow from the other shore. She had awakened, stepped into the reality of what a human could become, what they were intended to be, a living doorway of light into a world held captive by darkness. Her gaze rested not on the soldiers, but the creatures of Shadow. The largest of which simply smiled at her. Bain stood in a nearby tree observing. His large form nestled in the black shade of night. He was not ignorant of the foe before him. His dark eyes, fully reflecting the light emanating from her, danced in assurance of his victory. She was young. Ignorant of the stage of battle she had now entered. Bain, eager to be rid of her brightness, raised his hand and snapped his claw like fingers. A Leech raised its head from one of the men in the group. Answering its commander with a screeching cry the four-foot ghoul glistened in the light Oya cast on him. A spiritual parasite Leeches drained the purpose and joy for life out of men. Although capable of controlling will, they rarely did so. Their utmost desire was to feed. By now she had manages to produce a ray of light from her hand, yet did not know how to wield it. The light bent and bowed and Oya tried to flick it like a whip. She lashed out with it toward the Leech, as it drove its host toward her.

Unable to see the flaming warrior Oya had become, the Sackeens stepped toward her. They spoke as if trying to quiet a frightened horse. "Come on girl; just let us get this over with." Oya was far from frightened, she was enraged, and had plunged into a fight beyond her experience. She missed directly hitting the Leech again and again. Her actions were not dislodging it from its post. Instead she only succeeded in making it angry. It sought to stop the speech that was pouring from her lips. Hissing at her with its gaping mouth it wrapped itself tighter around its host. The man lunged with impressive strength and knocked Oya to the ground. As he held her to the ground the Leech flung itself onto Oya. The other men cheered at their comrade's success in restraining her. The large dark mouth of the Leech covered her face. Its body bulged and heaved as it snuffed out her light. The fire that had shown throughout her members so brightly began to fade. Her limbs stopped moving and she lay still. The brand was brought out and searing pain brought her back to her senses. The Leech had left her, as she sat up she trembled from over exertion. She was dragged to the nearest tree where the men began to whip her for her rebellion.

Having no more strength to fight, or even to call for help, her spirit was the only thing that could cry, and her cry was heard.

It was at this time that a small group of fishermen appeared on the road coming around a bend near the house. Upon seeing them, the soldiers paused in their flogging. The leader of the group of lowly Sea Folk stepped forward and spoke. His words and manner instantly caught everyone's attention. "You should be more careful which such a gift." The soldiers, still heated in a hostile state, did not know what to make of him. They were growing tired of the nights work. Each man wondered if they were up to taking on a group of grown men. It was a dark night; there was no way of telling how many Seamen stood out of sight. The Captain of the soldiers re-collected himself first and stepped up to meet the usurper face to face. "Move on, Seaman, or your fate will be worse than hers." As the Captain said this he took a step and moved as if to push the man away with the end of his spear. The fisherman looked from the Sackeen to the spear and back again with amused surprise. The Seaman's expression seemed out of place. The unarmed Sea Farer appeared to believe that the Captain's weapon was punitive and such a confrontation beyond the soldier's abilities. The Captain, now uncertain, withdrew and stood rather dumbly waiting for the man and his friends to move on. They did not. Instead the other Sea Farers stepped up beside their leader. This appeared to the Sackeens to be an offensive move, but an astute observer would have acknowledged that they simply wanted to have a closer look at what was about to happen. They were students and this man was there teacher. The soldiers, in turn, stepped up behind their Captain, hoping more than believing, that the image of their collective force would in some way persuade these men to move on. Although the Sackeens were warriors, with superior training, whose armies harnessed the strength of creatures such as dragons and the greater fairy folk, Sea Folk braved the Sea. The men of the Shore were known for courage and strength. The delicate balance of power in this country rested upon the armies and political powers. Few Sackeens were stupid enough to take on a healthy fisherman man to man.

Oya had been dropped on the ground. Left unguarded she sat up weakly and looked around. She was still *Seeing*. She gasped and watched a large form come out of the shadow of a nearby tree and place itself among the company of soldiers. Bain had watched the scene with interest, but no alarm before now. Following him dark creatures seemed to crawl and lurch out of every shadow, as if being pulled against their own will. Oya looked at the strange man who had brought her relief. Unable to see clearly in the dim firelight his face eluded her. Darkness seemed to have overtaken the yard. Her neck burned but she could not escape the vision before her. Twisted forms, devoid of light, trembled as if in pain and uncertainty. They began to spit and hiss at the man, "We know who you are! Have mercy on us!" They cried. Their moans were horrible to hear and Oya tried to cover her ears, but it was no use, she could not muffle their horrible sounds.

The man on the road stood unmoving before the soldiers and Shadows. A type of pity came over his face, as his gaze fell upon the soldier who carried the Leech. Oya saw white light flicker across his face, as if a curtain were parted for a split second. The soldier went into convulsions and fell to the ground, then lay motionless. The Leech let go of him and writhed in pain as it cried out, "*Merrccyyy!*" She watched with wide eyes as it dissolved into the earth. Fear began to spread through the rest of the soldiers as they shifted their weight while gripping their spears; glancing back and forth to each other uncertainly. To them it appeared as if the stranger had just killed their friend with a glance.

The following silence was shattered as the Sea Farer's voice rose into the night air. "Let there be Light!" Oya was amazed as she saw trumpets raised in the air above him, and it seemed as if light came out of his mouth as well rather than just the sound of the word. She heard no sound but saw light blast out of them like torrents of wind. Even the small flame within her chest flickered in answer to the call. Instantly the scene changed. Rays of light sprouted up all around. Great glowing swords of all different hues were unsheathed. They were in the midst of the soldiers, around them, and in the trees. Great warrior type beings that moved and quivered as living fire appeared and attacked. Bain and his subordinates violently disappeared, with great shrieks of rage, accusing Him of an unmerciful onslaught. It happened so quickly, that Oya was still the midst of an exclamation of surprise when she realized it was over. Before her the soldiers lay on the ground stunned. One by one they picked themselves up and ran away. Once the yard was clear an empty stillness filled the place. A ripple of astonished laughter rumbled through the men, who all looked at their friend with faces aglow with awe.

The first man smiled at his companions and then looked over to Oya. He walked determinedly toward her and her eyes widened as she Saw a white light all about him. The brightness behind him left his face in shadow. He took her by the hand and helped her to her feet. His Light faded from her view. Now able to see his face, she was amazed to see nothing out of the ordinary. He was not ugly, neither was he strikingly handsome. He wore a short beard, which was stuck to his neck with dried sweat. His dress was plain and dirty. The aroma of salt and fish hung around him. She realized that he and his friends must have docked their boat at sunset after a day on the water. All of these realities sunk her into a silent stare. For some reason she was astonished to see a mere human being standing in front of her. His smile warmed her heart and something about him seemed very familiar. She could not help herself, and smiled faintly back at him forgetting the pain of her neck. He brushed some dirt off her shoulder "Well, baby sister, you did alright! Next time be sure to wear your armor when you fight. Courage like yours should be coupled with wisdom." He had an unassuming air, full of confidence and good nature, which was somehow mingled with a sorrow Oya did not understand. She looked down embarrassed. He lifted his head and laughed, as if he knew what she was thinking and found it amusing. The sound rolled through the air. She felt gentle waves of joy brush against her. Her glow within intensified when she heard it. She looked up at him and managed a very timid, "Thank you."

His eyes then fell to the burn on her neck. Deep hurt and concern flooded his face. Tears brimmed in his eyes, and Oya thought they looked like waves about to crash on the shore. Oya watched his face as hurt, anguish, anger, and love seemed to move across it in waves. She stared at him, unable to speak. He looked directly into her eyes, "The darker the night becomes, the closer you are to the dawn; and the end is a new beginning." His voice was soft, spoken only for her ears. The words resonated through her, making a lasting imprint, even though she was unsure of his meaning. The soldier that had been guarding Oya's parents emerged from the house. The stranger noticed him and called, "I believe your friends left without you." The guard ran off and Oya's parents came out. Rala grabbed her daughter and cried out in despair. Her mourning tones rang out and were heard in the houses of their neighbors.

The men stayed and spoke with Samuel into the night. Rala dressed her daughter's burn and whip marks with great sobs. Oya accepted her emotional embraces in shocked silence. What she had seen would not soon fade from her memory. The mark of Death on her seemed a little matter. She was now acutely aware that something of a much grander scale was occurring. She was determined to sit with her father and listen to the man speak. She stayed awake long to enough to learn that his name was Barduuk. He spoke of his father and of the Sea and the mysteries beyond. At the time Oya did not understand much of what he said as she sat on the floor and listened to him. Her face showed her exhaustion and he glanced at her and his eye twinkled as he winked. An undeniable peace moved over her as she heard His voice and she drifted off into a quiet sleep as she laid her head on her father's knee.

All by herself, Aylia had slipped away during the night. Unnoticed to the rest of the world Aylia sought out the words of the waves. She had found a place out of sight under a large dock. She put the sorrow and darkness of the night behind her and listened as she watched the water. Sitting cross-legged on the cool sand she opened her heart to the voice of the Sea. It seemed dense tonight, as though it carried something burdensome. She barely had to listen to hear it. The water sang, a song--a rolling melody of love and comfort. Though it had a melancholy ring to it, Aylia heard the sound of laughter. Mingling within sorrowful tones she heard a joyful sound of hope. Closing her eyes the singing voices enveloped her. Great tears flowed down her cheeks. Warm drops of water felt like gentle fingers caressing her face. A great pressure filled her until she began to heave sobs of release. She mourned her fate. She felt a great emptiness, as if there was a place in her heart that had never felt as it was meant to. The doom before her threatened all hope that someday that need would be satisfied. She had thought for so long that the key to her longing would be found later in life. With an unwanted death now set before her, she began to wonder if the meaning of her life lay not on this Shore, but in the next. Uncertain of what she was longing for; she opened her eyes and watched her tears slip from the tip of her nose onto her wrists, trail over her skin, then, fall down into the sand. She thought of her tears as they fled from her pain, contemplating their escape from her sorrow as they now returned to the Sea. She envied them. Her heart longed to be free as well, to be joined with something that called to her from an unseen Shore. The nettling suspicion she had always had, that something was out of place, that things didn't fit just as they should was rising up again. She thought for a long time about what might be missing, what could change the violent world she was a part of.

Her nose tingled with the salty smell of the water. Coolness hugged her bottom and legs as she sat in the damp sand. The crashing of the waves moved through her head and spun around the questions in her mind. She gazed at the moonlit waves. Hope seemed like the light that hung in the dark sky. It appeared so perfect, an unblemished sphere in the heavens. The same light, however, was shattered to pieces as it fell on the rolling waves of her world. White points of light danced on dark waves in the distance. Aylia noticed how bright each wave seemed, how the many points of sparkling light on the water were more eye catching than the single moon above. *Perhaps,* she thought, *we are the waves, each asked to be one little point of light. That's what I'll do, I'll*

reach up toward the light, like the waves do, and not focus on the dark water
below.

And that night, for the first time, Aylia heard another voice. It was not the ringy voice of the shallows; this was deeper, resonating through the waves. She was sure she had not heard it before. Yet, she felt as if it were an old acquaintance, long forgotten. She turned her head as she listened, not daring to believe at first, *"Aylia! Aylia!"* The richness of the presence reached in and filled the abyss that lay at the core of her being. A dull thundering, a voice full of unfathomable depth that made even the Sea sound shallow, called to her. Part of her, not bidden by the memory of her mind, remembered the sound. And she knew she was not alone.

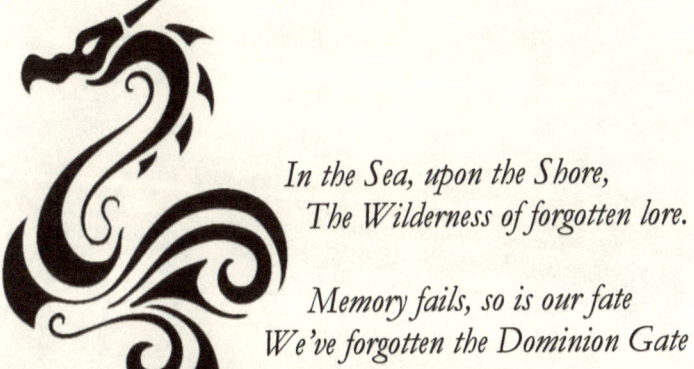

In the Sea, upon the Shore,
   The Wilderness of forgotten lore.

Memory fails, so is our fate
We've forgotten the Dominion Gate

4

Plunging into the Sea, Malice used his great wings to push himself down through the water to the seabed. He was a spirit of the air, and moving through water was work for him. The journey was not long, as Shadows travel, and he soon set down before a Gate that lies in the Sea. Immense before him two living creatures stood guard at the portal to the dimension of Shadows. Their front claws just touching on the ocean floor and their immense wings were stationed tip-to-tip above; nearly touching beneath the glow of the surface were the water tinted blue rather than black. In between them a wall of liquid incandescence appeared to quiver gently with the currents of the water. The unfeeling eyes of the guardians penetrated Malice as he moved. Upon entering he passed beyond the mortal realm into Darkness. Here his form could be fully realized. He stood tall and fearsome just emerged from the gateway. Great whirlwinds moved in a violent dance of color. Puffs of red steam and flickers of flame were the forms of Furies moving to and from the land of men.

There seemed to be much movement going on. He was suspicious that word had reached his master of Bain's defeat. Malice had resolved not to report on that front until he had more information. The Fury traveled through the many corridors of the fiery labyrinth until he came to the centermost chasm and was confronted by a great divide. Malice bent over and rested his presence on his knuckles and waited. Materializing on the opposite cliff his master called his name. Fiery embers danced as a being more spirit and flame than flesh became visible. He unwound his coils as if awaking from slumber. Orange and gold were entwined within every scale. Red light escaped like flames from his armor as he moved. A haunting laughter resonated through the deep. "Malice, do get up. Too much humility is not becoming for one such as you." The voice exhibited an intelligence that was a lovely mingling of ancient knowledge and present understanding. Malice had no wish to look up. This was the Prince, the First of the flame serpents. He cowered before the power of the creature. Ophinum had been his name in the beginning, though none dare to speak it. The truth of his form goes beyond what men can perceive. The great cylinder of flames and scales, appearing like jewels, faded away. Malice glanced up as a more tangible figure seated himself on the immense throne which sat on a cliff above.

"I believe, Malice, that some of your subordinates had an encounter recently with," he paused as if searching for the right word, then smiled as if amused by some secret joke he did not need to share with his servant ". . . a Man." Malice dared to look across the great pit before him. His master spoke with an easy tone, as if he was speaking of something trivial. Malice's eyes were drawn to the set of Keys his master fingered on the end of his scepter. He had no fear of the key of Death, while it was in the serpents keeping. Ophinum was not a creator, he could not wield that power over anything other than flesh, but to a Fury the key to Hades posed a threat. His master *could* lock him away in that abyss. Malice shuddered in fear of the one who ruled him. Great eyes of deep embers recaptured Malice and bore deep into his being. Ophinum spoke on, "Malice, I have brought you here, to educate you."

Malice left the inter-dimensional dominion shaken, but with no more information than when he had arrived. He had been given orders, not information, "Stay away from the man, and do not get in his path." He was one Ophinum would deal with himself, at a "*more opportune time.*" Malice growled as he moved through the earth. Whatever this man's purpose was at least he would not have to deal with him. Still he felt no relief. Two small creatures hovered around him as he made his way back to the Shore country. They were Eyes, and their talents would allow Ophinum to see what took place in Malice's territory, since the Man had now traveled there. Malice wondered what his lord was expecting to see.

Back in the chasm, Ophinum sat alone, fingering the keys that hung from his scepter. Though he bore no wounds, Ophinum had been defeated in his own encounter with the Man months before. He would wait. His plan caused a faint smile to appear on his lips. Wait until this Man was at his weakest point. Then he would return to him. The corners of his mouth twitched as he ran his finger over the key of Death. Its ethereal craftsmanship quivered under his touch. There was no power greater that could be wielded against flesh and blood. And if this mortal resisted him again, Ophinum would unleash Suffering and unlock Barduuk's Death.

We cannot know, the Gates are barred
Stolen from us, by the fallen stars

We did not guard, we did not keep.
Our days wax on, we fall asleep.

Basking in the light of youth
He crept in as the greatest sleuth.

Seeking what we might
Rise and gain
His triumph is
Our darkest shame.

The Keys were forged, in hope to wait
Needless did we enter the Gate

The speech was fair, the form divine
Beauty and evil intertwined

We grasped to take what was our share
Glory stripped, our sin laid bare

The Serpent rose to claim our right
Naked and cold, we had no Sight

The Gates were shut, the Doors were locked,
From men to Light, the way was blocked.

He comes to die, to take our plight
To keep the Keys, the Dark will fight

But Victory belongs to Him
Who comes and goes, to come again.

Listen children, turn your ears,
Wisdom comes, so have no fear

Mysteries lost will yet unfold
You cannot say, you were not told.

5

Oya stepped out of the darkness within her house and into the morning light. Squinting against the brightness it took her a moment or two to before she saw her father sitting on the large boulder, which sat off to the side of their home. He was holding his sitar and gazing over the grassy fields that were being gently rolled by the wind. The Sea lay beyond and the Veil glowed brightly in the morning light. Oya could hear his deep voice as she approached, he was singing. It was a song few bard's cared to sing anymore, but it had always been one of Samuel's favorites. She climbed the rock and sat next to him. When her father sang, a wonderful atmosphere surrounded him, enveloping those nearby in an aura of warmth and light that penetrated deep into the heart. This was Samuel's gift. A deposit from the Other shore, purposed to reveal its mysteries through music. Samuels voice rose, playfully carried high by the wind. Oya loved the sound. The music touched her in a new way as her heart was now altered by the knowledge of impending sorrow.

When the song was over Oya and her father sat in silence. Each pondering a future they did not wish for. Oya's thoughts drifted to the Veil as she looked at it. *What does it keep us from seeing?* She wondered. And she thought about the old tales. Of times when men knew of the other dimensions, before the Gates were barred. Men had let go of the knowledge of portals. No one spoke now about actually seeing the other shore or what lived there. The word mystery was swimming around Oya's head. The Other shore was a mystery. What would she see; when through death she achieved the other shore? Was there a purpose behind her mark? She sat back pulling one of her knees up and sighed as she wrapped her arm around it. Reflected in her blue eyes the sky was open and wide, and no death or doom was could be seen.

"Papa," she said in a feathery dreamy voice that was full of depth. "What do you know of the Gates?" Samuel chuckled just a bit as he set his instrument down. The subject had always been of interest to him and he had devoted many hours of his time to the study of it. In his youth he had poured over the Chronicles of the Oracles and Seers, the writings that were not openly read to the public, but kept for the study of the 'elect' in the temple. He had visited the library often when he had studied under the Sage. The wise man was gone and Samuel smiled at the memory of his old teacher. "There are no specific teachings about portals." He began, "The Gates are mentioned, one in the Sea, one upon the shore and another which lies in the wilderness. At first I was led to believe the only difference between a Gate and a portal was their size and fame. But the more I studied the more I came to understand that a Gate was more than just a doorway from one dimension to another. A Gate was where the two dimensions could actually overlap, both realities realized in the same place. Whereas portals are more like open windows, which allow the light of the other shore to shine here. Yet, the real mystery of portals or Gates lies in the keys that open them."

Samuel became lost in his thoughts; the vision of a young woman filled his mind. He smiled, "I believe I saw an open portal once." Oya looked at her father, he seemed miles away. She recognized the glimmer in his eyes, he was thinking of his life before her and her mother, when he lived at the temple and studied under the Priests. The memory he thought of troubled him, as if he was still not comfortable with what he had seen. He suddenly felt the need to talk about it. "Women are not permitted to study in the temple," he stated, "they are only allowed serve, for that reason prophetess' are…. rare." He sighed, as if he was digging up treasures long forgotten. "She worked in the temple, hungry for any insight and knowledge she could obtain. I've never seen such a scrawny little waif of a thing." He looked down as he smiled at an unseen glimpse into his past. "And no one paid her much mind. She was quiet but something about her intrigued me." He lifted his hands and motioned as he talked as if trying to materialize his memory in some way. "She always carried a little wrap of leather that held paper. I assumed that she wrote down what she heard in the temple, you know, took notes of the teachings. Well, one day she dropped a piece of paper and I happened to find it." His eyes squinted as if he was trying to bring the memory into better focus. "On it were drawings of many things; strange figures and creatures that were not from this world." Samuel looked down as if lost in thought. Oya prodded him on, "What happened to her?" A tender smile came across his face. "I followed her that day; I wanted to return her drawing to her, down through the tunnels and chambers beneath the Temple. And I found her, sitting alone in a little room, long forgotten. She was squatting down in front of a wall, with a paintbrush in her hand. I saw on the wall in front of her an open door, a round bubble of golden light that moved like water. Her face was illuminated with a dance of color, as if she was standing before a liquid mirror that was reflecting the sunlight. And just for a moment, I thought I saw someone standing on the other side of that bubble of a door. He was like a man made of light, and... he smiled at me. Yet he was fierce, like a white tiger of a man. He faded from my view as she sensed my presence and stood up. I had startled her and she dropped her brush. I then saw what she was painting, beautiful pictures of woods and nature, with such wonderful expressions of light. What she had painted was amazing. It was if she had visited the other Shore. She was afraid I would expose her little haven, but I never did."

The sound of a twig breaking made them both turn around. Oya's mother stood behind them. She gave a motherly smile to Oya. "Honey, would you mind doing the milking for me today?" Oya hopped off the rock casting a sideways smile at her father as she took the bucket from her mother's hand and walked off. Rala turned her face and watched her daughter until she was out of sight in the shed. When she faced Samuel again her cheeks were wet with tears. "I wished you had told me, Samuel." Rala voice trembled under the pressure of much emotion. Samuel's face showed his surprise; as he realized she must have been standing there for a while. Tears began streaming down her soft face. When Samuel had found her that day painting alone in the darkness, her life had forever changed. They had become friends and found in each other kindred spirits who were aware of the presence of Light ebbing at the shore of men...Months later Samuel had heard discussions of the room that had been found in the tunnels, filled with images of evil creatures where no doubt a witch was hiding. Samuel had feared for her safety and they had fled. Rala had never known the power inherent in her gift. When Oya had come to them, she had put those things aside. At the time they had known of no other way to survive, than to hide away. He wondered now if he should have encouraged her more to continue in her art of revealing. Rala and Samuel talked for over an hour. On why these things were resurfacing now, and why Oya had been marked. As they spoke Samuel began to wonder if the Sackeen's were being used to wipe out those who showed Gifting. He couldn't imagine how the Seekers could hunt for such gifts, but it could be possible. He kept such ideas to himself for the time being, his thoughts were just running wild. He had no real basis for such an assumption, did he?

I tell you, I know
The truth only flows

To ears that will hear
Unbound by fear

You look but don't see
Any hope now for me.

6

Aylia's mother, Rapha, rose early after not sleeping well. Her heart was in turmoil. Disbelief and shock numbed her. What was to become of her daughter? Was there any hope now? If they tried to flee, their village would be turned over to dragon's fire. Rapha shook herself, refusing to mourn, yet. Visions filled her head of her mother comforting a woman whose child had been slain. Her mother's words comforted her now, "The King will do as he promised. Our tears are only for a little while. Comfort will come. Let your heart grieve, but do not give into despair. Our hope is across the Sea." Rapha's heart was in turmoil. What good was a King across the Sea while their children died on this shore? She looked over and watched Aylia as she slept. Her child seemed so peaceful. Rapha walked over and brushed the hair off of her forehead and kissed her gently. She stood up and straightened her back in solemn resolve. Yesterday had been a dark day, but today would be better. She put on her shawl and grabbed her basket. She would go to the market and get some air. Some fresh fruit, Aylia's favorite. Death would soon darken their doorway soon enough, but not today. Rapha opened the door silently and stepped outside.

Each step was calculated with brisk determination. As if each one took her further from her daughter's misfortune. As she neared the village the road began to get crowded. Rapha frowned and looked around. She had hoped for the early calm of the morning in the town. As she examined those around her, etched upon the faces that dared to look upon her she saw great pity and sorrow. Low murmurings and hushed voices swam around her like the buzzing of bees. The village was disquieted; this turn of fortune had brought with it a thick cloud of doubt and fear. No one felt safe; the reality of their subjection to Sackeen rule had been thrust into their faces once again. Many women turned from her as she passed, afraid that the rush of relief they felt that their own children had not been chosen might show. A crowd of sad faces spun around her. She wondered where the others were. How many fathers would perform the burial rights over empty graves? She hoped that the other mothers, although separated by geography, would like her; realize that they did not suffer alone. Rapha looked at the sky in an attempt to escape from the faces that reminded her so keenly of their misfortune. Red clouds hung in golden light as the sun continued to climb over the mountain. The silhouettes of gulls passed overhead. In a flash she saw the small shapes of the birds replaced by the dark figures of dragons. She shivered and tried to pull away from the vision. How long? How long?

When Rapha returned to the house and was nearly to the door, it swung open wildly and she was nearly bowled over by her son. Koim was taller than his father, though he was more slender. Unlike Aylia who was all light and joy, Koim was a serious young man for nineteen. He had been out night fishing. His blonde curly hair, only a shade lighter than Aylia's, hung down over a stern glower that shadowed his eyes. It lightened only for a moment as he stooped to help his mother pick up the basket she had dropped when he had burst out on her. "Koim, honey, it's all right. Now just let me get it." Koim was angry. "I should have been here!" He shouted as he threw the fruit into the basket, nearly ruining it. Rapha drew in a breath as she stood and gave her son a stern motherly look. "I'm very glad you weren't here son." Koim had always been impulsive and passionate. "No doubt you would have tried desperately to help, but I fear your good intentions would have only caused you to join your sister in her fate." He leveled his eyes at her. She was right of course. He looked out toward the Sea. When he looked back to his mother his eyes were wet and sadness had washed away all traces of anger. "She's so young mom." Rapha reached up and hugged the man before her with the same tender embrace she had given him when he was four. "It's alright, Koim. I don't know how, but we have to believe that it will turn out all right." Rapha nearly sobbed hoping she could believe the words she herself had spoken. Koim straightened himself out of his mother's arms. He looked off again forcing his words out as he struggled to control his emotions. "She's not even crying. She seems almost happy. She's in there talking about a conversation she had at the shore last night. That she knows she can bear this weight, because she doesn't have to bear it alone." He looked back at her incredulously. The world seemed to have turned around two times in one dark night. He covered his face with his hand and squeezed the tears from his eyes. He kissed his mother on the cheek and stepped out into the untamed field behind their home. It would take time for him to come to terms with this. 'Why her?' he thought to himself as he walked. 'What happened? Why didn't father fight?' Although Koim believed that there was a king across the Sea, his faith in this had not yet grown into reliance, especially for such an immediate need. No, he needed to do something. He only knew one thing for certain; he would find a way to save her. Rapha looked after him with a heavy sigh and entered the house.

Six months later, Koim was sent out to find Aylia, again. She had always been fond of long solitary walks, but in the past she had never failed to tell her family where she was going and when she would return. Concern for her whereabouts was increasing as rumors were spreading that the Sackeen preparations were nearly complete and the Riders would be coming to collect the marked ones soon. Koim was making quick strides through the tall grass. His concern and fear for his beloved sister was mingled with his misunderstandings. He was becoming angry and resentful of her apparent incapacity for understanding their parents need to have her nearby. He knew where he would find her. Somewhere along the shore, listening to her *water words!!* Koim understood that perhaps with the approaching doom before her, Aylia needed to escape at times, but he could not forgive her for seeming to prefer the company of the Sea to her own family. She had wondered off today shortly after noon, and now sunset was drawing near and she still had not returned. Every time he searched for her he was terrified that he would not find her. That she would be taken while they were unaware.

As he strode out of the bushes onto the sandy shore he saw her. He exhaled. She had walked up the beach and was sitting all alone gazing out at the waves. He was still a ways away, but he tried to call to her. She didn't seem able to hear him so he began walking up the sandy bank. She looked so peaceful and content. How could she be so when her mother was at home sick with fear that she had been lost forever? He could not bear to see his mother cry. Although he knew in truth that Aylia was not to blame for her situation, he was preparing to lay into her for her absent-minded absence. By the time he was near enough to call to her, she had stood up and turned to look at him as he approached. He stopped short. Her lovely face was streaked with tears, which glistened like golden jewels in the evening light.

She smiled at him and her face sparkled. Koim stared at her for a moment, lost in the beauty of the vision before him. Trying to find the little girl that was his sister in the Seafaress he saw before him. The wonder of his gaze reminded Aylia of her tears and she quickly wiped her face. Koim stepped forward and took her by the shoulder, "Are you alright, Aylia?" She wiped the water from her eyes onto her dress. "Oh, yes." She glanced up at him with a slight smile, embarrassed that he had seen her intimate moment of emotion. His concern confronted her abashment, "You know you've been gone for nearly five hours, mother's beside herself. It's time to come home for supper." Aylia's mind, in part, was still across the Sea, but Koim's words helped her come back to this Shore. "Dear mother," she said looking thoughtfully toward the water. She looked back to Koim, "I'm sorry, I've simply been losing track of the time lately." She took one more longing glance at the Veil before turning toward home. She began to step gracefully through the long grass and her brother moved in step next to her. His brow was furrowed. He could not understand her. "Aylia, what is it about the Sea, that touches you so you forget your own mother?" Aylia looked at him, hurt by the sting of his words. "It's not that I forget my mother" she replied, "but that I remember *Him.*" "Him, who? The king?" Koim spoke briskly. "Yes." She replied.

"Aylia, I know people used to hear the water words, but they just don't any more. The men who did were the great kings and Oracles of the old days, and I doubt very much that the King would speak directly to a simple maid from across the Sea."

Aylia allowed herself a bit of a laugh, "That's just what I said to Him."

"What do you mean?" Kiom stopped and looked at her squarely. Aylia tried to explain, "I know that we've never thought that we could ever actually speak with the King. We've all been taught the general understanding that the King would simply come back one day and over throw the Sackeens to retake the throne. We are taught ceremonious chants to pay our respect to His authority, but we never dare to actually speak to Him. We've contented ourselves with the belief that we simply need a better ruler. But the One across the Sea is not like we are; he is. . . much….. more. Oh, Koim, I just can't wait until you meet him." Aylia let herself get taken away for a moment and she began to rattle on like a little girl. She grasped her brother's hand wishing so much to share what she knew and felt with him. "Oh Koim, if you only knew how much he cares. He's just waiting to go fishing with you, he told me so today. He wanted me to tell you he'll be waiting for you at your favorite spot. He says you know the place. …"

Koim cut her off, "Were did you hear that non sense? A great, All Knowing, All Powerful, Lightbeing wants to go fishing?" Aylia would not be swayed, "He told me so himself, don't you have a secret fishing place? That only you know about?"

A torrential rushing sound interrupted their conversation. Koim and Aylia looked up together. In the sky, silhouetted against the deepening pink and red of the sunset, two dragons flew overhead. Koim and Aylia watched them as they glided southward down the shore. Koim shivered as he watched. Sackeens used the dragon riders to collect those chosen. Aylia knew this as well, however, this was her first time seeing dragons flying this close and the sight of them filled her with awe.

Koim, on the other hand, was filled with fear. He shook his head, and answered his sister's question in fearful anger, "NO! I don't, I don't know what you're talking about! There are bigger more important things going on! Aylia," his voice broke and he turned toward her, his eyes looking for hope, but drowning in the despair. "People are dying, and are going to die, YOU are going to die!" He stopped and looked down, ashamed of himself for speaking this out loud. Aylia stepped close to him and touched his shoulder lovingly.

"Koim, look at me."

He raised teary eyes. "I'm not afraid."

Aylia was smiling. She was growing in confidence because she now understood how fragile life was. She didn't know how much longer she had to share these treasures with Koim. He turned and ambled off without her. He looked around hopelessly unable to talk anymore. He saw his sister, the concern and understanding on her face, yet he could not get past her age. A little girl could not know such things.

Aylia watched him as his legs brushed through the grass with each step. He had grown so serious lately. She understood that one cannot keep all the carefree whiles of youth, but Koim had lost all joy. Although her circumstances established for her a certain death, she was still going to live and love toady. For Koim it was as if a part of him, the best part had already died. He moved as if he carried a heavy burden, one that was not his to bear.

If you could run,
  Would you not flee?
    In the dark,
      Do you not See?

      Pain will come,
    And pain will go
  But in the end,
The truth will show.

7

Four days later Koim woke Aylia early in the morning. It was still dark out and the wind was blowing, bidding of a coming storm. "Aylia! Aylia, wake up." Koim was trying to whisper, but it was coarse. Aylia propped herself up in bed. "What's the matter?"

"Come on, we have to go." He threw her clothes at her. "Get up, get dressed."

Aylia began to reply, but Koim put his finger to his mouth for her to be quiet. He then turned and silently stepped out the door.

Aylia got dressed and followed him outside. It was warm out. The cool of fall had not yet crisped the air. The sky was just beginning to show the hints of the approaching dawn overshadowed by dark clouds. Koim was standing at the corner of the house. Next to his feet lay a large bundle. Aylia walked over, "Koim, what are you doing?"

"We're leaving."

Aylia understood. She looked at him in desperation. "Koim, no. Think of what they'll do to mother and father if I'm not found."

"Mother and father know. They want *you* to live. Now come on, we'll get to the docks of Navar. "

He threw a cloak over her shoulders and picked up the bundle. Taking her by the hand he spoke firmly, "Aylia, you are going to live a full life, not die a meaningless death."

She looked to the house, leaving just didn't feel right, not like this. Koim pulled her away before she could make any clear thoughts. As they scurried off Koim kept talking softly. "I'm sorry Aylia, sorry you couldn't say good-bye. It is better that they don't know when we left or where we are going."

That evening Aylia was sitting wrapped in her cloak next to the small fire Koim was warming his hands over. He looked around in the failing light. They had made good time despite the fact that they traveled through rugged areas rather than using the roads. They were both lean and fit, which helped. Aylia looked around uncomfortably. She was tired and gazed into the small fire as she tried to think. Koim was capable and determined. Yet, as she watched him she knew he was fearful and apprehensive.

"We should reach Navar tomorrow." He said as he pulled some bread from his pack. He broke it into pieces and gave thanks as he passed some to Aylia. She took it but set her hand down in her lap rather than taking it to her lips. She did not feel hungry. A strange unsettling feeling had been growing in her spirit all day. It was making her fidgety and grumpy. At first she had thought she was distraught over never seeing her parents again. Although this was true, she understood that survival meant sacrifice at times. No, this was something more. Koim noticed she was not eating and asked her if she was all right.

"I don't know Koim." She said it with some force and he raised his eyebrows in surprise. She regretted the tone of her voice. "I'm sorry." He just looked down and nodded. There had to be grace in a time like this. They were going through enough as it was. Aylia shuffled around a bit. She got up and paced, but nothing helped. Koim tried to speak to her again. "Aylia, you should try to get some rest."

"I know, there is no telling how long we'll be running for, is there?" She spun around and plopped herself back on the ground.

Koim looked down. The night sky was growing darker. It made the countless obstacles before them seem impenetrable. The unseen vapor like fingers of Fear and Doubt moved over the ground and began to grasp at their thoughts. They both knew that turning back would mean death for Aylia, but would going forward hold anything better for either of them?

On the cold hard ground of the earth that night, while the cares of her life were many, Aylia dreamt. She was in her house, packing, preparing to leave. She looked out the window and saw her parents, walking around. The ground was covered in snow. Aylia walked out of the house and toward them. As she did, the snow began to melt and the ground could be seen. A small animal sat behind a shed. A fence of twigs and thorns encased it. It was very small and white; covered in soft downy fir. Fine soft feathers ruffled its back. It appeared like a newborn. Aylia grabbed it, already feeling that she wanted to keep it, but not really knowing what it was. It looked a bit like a kitten, only larger. She picked it up and pulled it out of the thicket like fence. She sat and held it on her lap while she examined it. Its eyes and ears were sealed, much like young cats or dogs are. But she heard it speak. A voice she could hear in her head, feminine in nature. "*You will be there when I am to be sacrificed.*" Aylia wondered what that meant. As she held it, she came to realize that it was growing in her hands. Its nose, much like a cat's became long like a horse. Its ears opened and were pointed. Its feet grew and she realized this would be something similar, yet very different from a dragon. Large white wings opened. Aylia then *saw* her, the white creature, being tied down to a large stone table. It wailed and struggled as darkness held it fast. Then a man appeared, standing at the front of the table. His presence was vague to the eyes, but powerful in spirit. Aylia and the creature calmed down at his presence and the darkness receded. A burst of light from the clouds above caught Aylia's attention and she looked up and saw the sky part above her. It was as if she could see into another place. The creature was there in a heavenly realm. Light, powerful light was bursting forth all around her and she was grown and battle ready. Bursts of color, reds, purples and orange- yellow hues shone all around. The creature was clad in golden and silver armor that moved like flames in the light. Aylia watched in growing terror as the white beauty opened her mouth and revealed fearsome teeth. A trumpet kind of call came from her mouth, as if a precipice in time had been achieved. All creation shook in response to the call. The light began to pierce the clouds and Aylia broke herself out of the dream. She was sitting up trembling and sweating. Her heart was troubled by the intensity of the vision. Koim was already up and noticed her abrupt exit from her sleep. She wiped her face as she looked around. Sweat caused her hair to stick to her brow. Her brother walked over and touched her forehead. He worried she might have caught a chill. Aylia brushed his hand away.

"I'm alright," she said with a puzzled look. "It... it was just a dream."

They began moving as the sun rose. It was a dull morning. A gray sky hung overhead. The air was cool and hinted of coming rain. Koim led the way along a low ridge. It was not long before the city of Navar could be seen below. The Sea was rough and dark beyond the town. The scenery was picturesque even on a stormy day, but neither one of them were in a mood to appreciate it now. Koim seemed to find more strength and confidence with each step. He thought freedom was beaconing to them. Aylia trudged along behind her brother. She felt heaviness within her, growing with every step. There was a bit of excitement at the unknown, but the glimmer faded fast. She looked back for a moment and knew that even if she ever tasted true freedom, the bitterness of her families' fate would always haunt her. With every step her soul became more restless. She felt a presence within her, one she could not explain. It grew in intensity the closer they came to Navar. Aylia couldn't grasp the meaning of what she was feeling and her lack of understanding made her anxious. The presence penetrated deep within her chest. It felt as if another heart was with her beating along with hers. Another heart that was strong whose beat she could not only feel within her chest but in her soul. *Bum, ba, dum. Bum, ba, dum.* It grew in intensity until she gasped for her breaths and sat down in weakness. Koim turned and seeing her on the ground rushed to her side.

"Aylia, are you hurt? What's the matter?"

She felt as if her breath was shallow. It surprised her when she realized she was able to speak. "I, I don't know, Koim. I feel like my heart it going to beat right out of my chest." She had her hand on her chest, for the pressure was intense. She took slow deep breaths. Koim laid his hand over hers. He felt the deep fluttering that was occurring within her. He pulled back his hand quickly, "Aylia what's going on?"

"I don't know, Koim, it started faintly about a half an hour ago. It's just continued getting *deeper*, I guess would be the word. Just….let me…sit here for a minute and catch my breath. I'm not hurt, it feels like my heart will explode, but it's not, I can't explain it any more than that." Koim sat down beside her and put his hand on her back. When he touched her, though, the deep boom of the beats began tingling up his arm. He pulled back and sat a few feet away. Whatever it was, it made him feel uncomfortable. They were sitting on the last small rise of a hill before reaching the city. Aylia could see the Sea. She took a break from the journey and remembered the water words. She longed now to hear the tiny bubbly voices of the ripples. Closing her eyes, she smiled as she thought of them. A breeze lifted the hair from her face and she remembered the roar of the large waves, like so many lions daring the land of men to conquer them. She took in a deep breath, hoping for the salty see air to fill her nose. But the fish stink of the city was too strong. She opened her eyes and took in the scenery before her. Many wooden structures littered the shore. The sound of people filled her ears as they bustled about with so many murmurings and grumblings. She suddenly had no wish to enter the city.

She glanced at her brother. He had gotten up and was pacing around. Keeping guard, considering the dangers they could be facing. Her face softened at the sight of him. He was trying too hard, trying to save her. She loved him for his trying. The beating had subsided. It was still there down deep within her, but it had faded into the background of her form for the moment. She stood up, "It's feeling better now, Koim. I think I could go on now." Koim looked at her and silently nodded his head. He threw a small pebble to the ground with a type of finality and picked up his bundle. Aylia recognized the look on his face and bit her lip. He was set in his course. The last stretch of their journey into the city was walked in silence.

A meeting, a chance
One moment, one glance

One way or another
For a love like no other

8

Brown. Although Navar was a city by the Sea it was brown. Brown dirt streets, brown wood houses, even the faces of the people were brown, well weathered by the sun and the sea. As her brother moved her through the busy streets Aylia felt as if she was in a bubble. The reason for her journey, her struggles her pain, the comforting voice of the water, and the deep presence within her; all these things were like rungs on a fence that kept her apart from the people that she now walked among. Koim walked aimlessly. He wanted it to appear as if he and his sister were here to shop. A small group of Sackeen soldiers were standing at the corner of the street. As Koim and Aylia walked past, the watchful eyes of one of the soldier's passed over the two travelers. Koim's body trembled as he allowed himself a glance at the soldier as he took his sisters hand and moved on. The Sackeen returned to his conversation with his comrades.

The resonating pounding within Aylia's chest was returning. Every face she saw seemed to spur it on. She felt the pounding within her chest. Her heart beat within her like the footfalls of a galloping steed. Coming closer and louder the second heart beat within her rose; like another horse overtaking the first. For a moment they beat together, like the pounding of two horses running side by side until finally the second over took her. The pounding filled her chest; she clutched her brother's hand and leaned close to him.

"Koim, I think I need to sit down."

Koim looked at her, "We're almost there, Aylia." He wrapped his arm around her shoulders. He could feel her body pulsating with tiny tremors. This time he could not pull away from her. He craned his neck to see over the people in front of him.

"Aylia, we have to make it through town, do you think you can do that?"

Aylia managed to nod.

Koim and Aylia made their way through the people in the streets. Every face she saw filled her with urgency and a need that seemed to be connected to the pounding. She wished desperately she knew what she was to do. Lightening flashed and a loud thunder- clap exploded overhead and everyone flinched. The rain started slowly but continued to grow steadily heavier. Koim pulled Aylia along with him and trotted into an open door.

They were overcome by the wonderful smell of food. A savory aroma of fish and crab and all good kinds of seasonings tickled their noses. They were in an eatery that was filling fast as many others were attempting to escape the storm as well. Koim sat Aylia down at a table near an open window. She hugged herself and concentrated on breathing as Koim looked around. The place was crammed, he would have to go to the bar to get Aylia and himself something to drink and eat. He slid his large bundle under the table near Aylia's legs.

"I'll get us something to eat." He placed his hand on her shoulder and looked into her face. "You gonna be alright AyAy?" Aylia looked up and smiled at his use of her nickname. Koim was the only person in the world who called her that. He hadn't called her that since they were little, it had always been special to her and she had felt a tinge of sadness when he had grown out of the habit. She told him she would be fine. The pounding was in fact subsiding and she was feeling tired and hungry. He wove his way through the people to the bar. Aylia didn't care for crowds and turned her face toward the window and watched the rain pour down on a now empty brown street.

Koim reached the bar and stood tall as he placed his hands on the wooden counter. He was at the far end of the bar, and sitting to his left was an elderly gentleman, worn from many years on the sea. He had a beard that was a matted tangle of black and gray hair and sharp piercing eyes. It seemed as though his retirement from fishing consisted of his sitting at his regular perch of this eatery and entertaining himself with the people who came through. He eyed Koim with great interest. "You're not a local, are ya boy?"

Koim glanced at him not really wishing to discuss with anyone where he was from or where he was going. The owner of the place, a stout man with a white apron on bustled by. He handed Koim a jug of ale and told him his missus would be with him in just a minute. Koim took a long drink as if he had forgotten the old seaman's question. His observer would not be so easily put off. He leaned up on his bar stool closer to the present victim of his avid curiosity. "From one of the villages, are ya boy?"

Koim rolled his eyes just a bit; he had never liked being called boy. He glanced again at the man and nodded in hopes of being left alone. The acknowledgement of his presence only spurred the old goose on. "Have ya come to see the wizard?"

Koim looked at the man with puzzled annoyance. The man had sparked his curiosity.

"Navar has no wizard." Koim stated.

"Ah, but there's one now that's come to visit our lovely little bit o shore. He's been showing off signs and wonders all week. Got the whole community in an uproar he has. People been coming from all around to hear him speak. No doubt that's why you've come." He nodded and sat back as he returned his pipe to the indent is his lip, as if there was no doubt in his mind to the strange lad's purpose here. A short round woman with bright red hair tied up on top of her head, placed a plate of food in front of the old man. He glanced at it with marked resignation, "You sure didn't come here for Fanny's cooking."

Fanny gave her regular customer a sideways glance, "Now mind your manners Seger, or I'll have Briton turn you out so's our new clientele can have an enjoyable dining experience." She turned her attention to Koim. "Well, now, what can we get for you, sir." Koim ordered two meals and then glanced back over the dining room and saw Aylia was still sitting alone gazing out the window.

The old meddler pulled Koim's attention back. "I'll tell you to beware of wizard's boy; it ain't natural for men to have such powers." Koim took the bait this time. "What powers? What kind of a wizard is he?"

Back at the window Aylia leaned against the sill. She raised her large bright eyes and watched the water stream off the edge of the roof. She smiled at the living icicles as they spun and danced their way into the puddles below and listened to their voices.

The raindrops slapped against the earth with great, *Tap, tap, splat splat* again and again. *Tap, tap, splat, splat, tap tap, splat splat, tap tap*. It was like a drum beat, *Get back, who's that, he's here, He's back.* Over and over again, it was the base line. Nearer to her she tuned into the lighter fluttery song of the water running off the roof, running, rippling down, joining the puddles as they all eventually united in one great symphony of song. A song about Him. Aylia smiled as she listened, it felt good to hear the water words again. The sound was comforting and reminded her of calmer quieter times. She reached out her hand and let the water dance upon her open palm. *We run, we sing, we joy, we ring. Our song is here, our song is now, he is coming, to show you how.* A group of men sprinted up the street through the rain. Aylia pulled her hand in and turned to look up the street. She had understanding. They were speaking of the king. He was here, near. She looked up and down the street again and saw no one, at first. Then one man came out of a building up the street. Aylia's gaze was fixed on him and she couldn't explain why. He glanced up and down the street, the rain settling on him in large drops that soaked his shirt. He would soon be drenched through. Aylia could see his chest rise as he took in a deep breath of the wet air. He lifted his face into the rain and smiled.

Aylia watched as it appeared that he spoke to someone, but she could see no one else. Then he moved as if he heard someone tell him something. He smiled again and looked around, until his eyes fell on her. He smiled right at her and began walking up the street in the direction of the eatery. Aylia felt her shoulders pull up, she felt insecure under his gaze. It was as if he knew her, really knew her. She had a sneaking suspicion that he even knew her most secret thoughts. She felt as though this man knew her in a way no one could know her, on a level beyond normal levels of human communication. As he drew near Aylia stood up next to the windowsill. Aylia wondered if he would come into the eatery. It seemed that he might. Aylia smiled back at him. But when he got to the place in the road where he should have begun to angle toward the door, he kept on walking straight up it, even though his head turned so that he gave her one last pointed look and nodded his head in a type of salute. His smile seemed to melt from his face as he turned and strode up the road. She felt as if her heart was going to pull itself right out of her chest and flop up the road after him.

Koim let his full gaze rest heavily upon the old man. He had been willing enough to excite general suspicion about the visitor of wonder that had graced his home town, but was now proving to be reluctant in sharing any details. It didn't take Koim long to understand that this old coot did not have any real information about the man he had brought up. He spoke more on the general state of awe among the town's folk, and the stories he had heard from others, than from firsthand experience.

"Well, everyone knows these is dark times we're living in now boy. Our young ones being marked and our streets being overrun with magicians. He's a Sea Farer too. That I would live to see one of our people turn to the dark forces."

Koim straightened up. He wasn't sure he particularly cared for the way the old man talked around a subject, interjecting darkness and doom. Things were gloomy enough, he couldn't imagine what the gentleman's comments would be if he knew of Koim's flight with his sister. He glanced up toward the kitchen anxious for his food, while the old man took a few puffs on his pipe. A tiny glint of something twinkled in the back of Koim's mind. A faint memory, of knowledge of a time long past: of stories he had rarely heard of the times before when Arcadia had been free and the servants of the King had had the power to baffle even the most powerful of dark wizards. Koim furrowed his brow as he accepted that those days were over. He was drawn out of his thoughts as Seger, the old, began to speak about the marked ones.

"It's a shame about those young ones that are to be taken," he leaned in toward Koim and spoke softly, "I'd have no qualms meself about facing the wrath of our over lord, if it meant even one of those little ones could have a chance." He nodded a deep gratified bow of his head as if he was a truly noble creature for speaking such. Koim looked at the rows of glasses across from him on the far wall, trying not to show how the subject affected him. But he swallowed hard and a bead of sweat dripped down the side of his face onto his neck. Before he was collected enough to look toward the man again Fanny came bustling out of the kitchen, a plate in each arm. She set them down in front of Koim. He thanked her as he paid. He picked up the dishes and turned around carefully. He nodded a farewell to Seger and headed back toward the table. It was still crammed in the room and he had to weave this way and that and nearly tipped the food onto a few folks. He was nearly to the table by the window before he realized Aylia's chair was empty.

Boom.

Boom.

The pounding in her chest was back. A deep sounding, that no longer threatened to immobilize her, but had spurred her on. She had no idea if it was courage or fear that moved her. She was afraid: afraid of missing a chance, maybe her only chance, for something, something more. When he had walked by she had moved quickly. She didn't remember telling her feet to move, or her hands to open the door. She was simply going, going to him. She was nearly twenty feet behind him. The cold rain saturated her until numbness enveloped her and she stopped. She was so close to him. It had to be less than eight feet when she froze. Her mind went blank. She didn't know what she would say. She had heard the water, all the water around, giving honor to him as the king as he passed by. He had the authority of the Other shore. Her mouth opened but no sound came out. She stood alone in the rain, only feet from her hope. Every part of her inner being cried out to him; calling out for help, asking for him. Her hand reached out to him. The water glistened upon her bare forearm. Everything felt as though it slowed down.

Boom.

Boom.

It took only a moment for her heart to fall to the feet that now would not move. Then, as if he heard something in the air, he cocked his head ever so slightly and paused for a moment. He turned around and looked at Aylia with a strange expression of recognition and awe toward her. Aylia absorbed every angle of the scene before her. How easily it seemed for him to turn toward her. The sound of his steps in the mud as he came to her seemed to make footprints in her heart. She stood a soaked quivering little mouse of a girl. He stopped only four feet from her. Her heart took a moment to believe that he was actually standing there, looking at her with a quizzical smile on his face. A wave of warmth ran through her, a rush of the purest acceptance of what you've always hoped for was real. That everything you've dared to dream of could step from the immaterial to the material, and she entered a new place of revelation which had taken hold of her. And she realized that this was her parent, her brother, her King. Without any thought to what propriety might be due to this man she lunged toward him and wrapped her arms around his waist as if he was Koim. She sobbed as she felt his arms wrap around her the sweetest hug she had ever known. He then pulled her back ever so slightly and she looked up at him. Rain dripped down on her face from tendrils of hair that hung around his.

"Hello, little one." He said. Her eyes grew big. A bolt of light moved through her, hitting her mind and heart. There was only one place, one voice that had ever called her by that name; the Voice of the Deep. She was amazed. Now the voice was different, a voice of a man, yet the undercurrent within the voice was the same. As if it was the same, the same thought, the same love, simply being expressed through a different element. Her mind whirled with so many thoughts, yet felt empty at the same time. She wanted to ask him a hundred different questions at once. He looked down at her as if he would be interested in anything she uttered. She forced herself to speak the only thing she could grab on to. "What is your name?"

He let go of her and got down on one knee and looked into her tiny face. He smiled as he introduced himself. "I am Barduuk, and you", he paused as he took her hand and formed a cup that quickly filled with raindrops. He touched the water and it giggled as if he tickled it, he looked into her eyes and smiled as he enjoyed her face as she listened and watched, he continued, "you….. *listen*."

Koim dropped the plates and bowls on the table, spilling food all over. A man from a neighboring table spoke up, "Eh, your friend there stepped outside a bit ago." Koim bolted for the door. Worry and fear taking over all thoughts of remaining unnoticed by others. When he was clear of the door he stopped in his tracks. Aylia was ambling along the road back toward the eatery. She held her hands out, playing with the rain as if lost in a dream.

"Aylia!" Koim's voice seemed to bounce off of every raindrop. Aylia looked up at Koim. He strode into the rain toward her. She was drenched. He took off his outer shirt and wrapped it around her. "What are you doing out here? It's pouring, you're soaked through."

The storm lasted through the night and into the next morning. Briton and Fanny rented them a small room they had over the storehouse. They were bedding down for the night; Aylia was sitting on the stuffed bed of straw as Koim piled up some blankets on the floor for himself. The two of them were troubled and neither one really wanted to talk about it. Aylia sat back deep in thought gazing out the small window. There was nothing out there for her. The window seemed a tiny door into a black abyss of destiny. She would not be following Koim in an escape. She played with the ends of her hair. Her conversation with the son of the King had changed everything. Once she had made her decision the heaviness that had grown in her with each step from home had vanished. A gently soothing unexplainable peace had taken its place. It was the reason for the aloof hint of a smile that now graced her face.

Koim fumbled with the blankets. Short quick glances at his sister gave him no comfort. A busybody who had been in the eatery earlier had gotten Koim off to the side later in the evening and informed him that she had seen his sister talking in the street with the *wizard*. She tried to seem concerned for the safety of the young girl she had seen talking to the man, but her manners were too marked for Koim to miss completely that she had intended to find out more about them. "I don't hold with butting my nose into strangers business," she had said with her hand over her breast as if making a solemn vow of truth. "But it wouldn't hurt you to keep a wary eye on her now, lest she be under some kind of enchantment and try to do herself harm!" She had batted her eyes at him as if she was ten years younger than she was, dipping her head as she tried to read his face for any expression that might lead her to understand how her heartfelt concern was being received. Koim could only give her a stern concentrated look. She had left unsatisfied, her attempts at civic duty had gained her little information about the young man and the girl with him. He didn't care for her manner or for the information she had given him. He was concerned enough for Aylia. He had watched her all evening, and had to admit that she did seem altered. Physically she appeared to be feeling better than before, but her eyes held a distant far off stare that troubled him. Although he had questioned her about why she had gone out in the rain she offered no explanation. Aylia had never been secretive and he could not understand why she did not tell him of her conversation with the stranger.

Aylia lowered her eyes. She took a deep breath as one hand played with a strand of hair that hung just below her shoulder. She heard the last words Barduuk had spoken to her. The deepness of the truth of his words gave her strength. "Be brave, little one. You do not know how strong you are, but you will soon see." Aylia breathed in deeply. "Koim." She had said his name without looking up. He stopped rummaging through their bag and looked at her. She forced her eyes to look at him. He sat across the small dusty room on his knees. He was a beautiful mess. His hair was tussled and he needed a bath. Aylia smiled at the straight strands of hay that hung from his curly hair. She thought of telling him he needed a good scrub, but the hopeful expression on his face did not permit her to put off the subject any longer. "Koim, I met the son of the King today."

She had spoken softly with a dreamy look in her eyes. Koim's brow furrowed and he stood up and looked at her closely. "The son of the King? Is that what he told you?"

Aylia thought about the question and realized that he had not said that of himself.

"No, he didn't say it, I just know it. And the water knows it." Aylia answered matter-of-factly.

"The water? All right. Well what did the man say to you?" Koim spoke out of concern.

"Koim, I can hardly put it to words. It's as if all my life I have seen the sun in the sky, a great burning round ball, out of my reach, yet feeling its warmth. Then imagine if one day the sun wanted to come down and meet us, so it sent a single ray of its light, to become a man. Then meeting the sunlight, standing right before me as a man, feeling that same warmth, I've always known, yet being able to touch it and speak to him now as a person. I don't think words can express it."

Koim rolled his eyes. He sat down near Aylia, "Sweety, listen to yourself, you're not making any sense. Did the man say something over you, a spell perhaps? Are you sure you're thinking for yourself?" He reached out to touch her face, but she pulled back. She stood up and moved around the room. Heat filled her. And tears threatened began to sting in her eyes, hot tears of hurt and anger. She struggled to find words. "A spell? You think I'm under a spell? No, I'm finally free from the spell, the one where we began thinking that we were wise enough to make a life or death decision on our own."

Koim looked up at her, not knowing what to say. "Koim, do you think that maybe there is something bigger than just me, or you going on here?"

Now Koim looked down. There was truth here, but he felt she was twisting it against him. He hardened his jaw and looked away. "Koim, I can't leave."

Now Koim lost his temper. "You will leave, even if I have to drag you across the country! No mind trap will draw you into giving yourself up to a Sackeen devil!!"

Aylia took a deep breath, "There are no other god's Koim who can take my life, unless the King gives them permission." She paused, it was no use arguing. Koim knew the truth, even if he would never admit it. Many before had tried to flee, and the consequences had been disastrous for those they left behind. There was no waste in giving up one's life for his friends and family. There is in fact was no greater act of love. Aylia had great love for those around her. Koim knew this.

"You know me, Koim, and that's why you never asked me if I wanted to escape. You drug me away before I had ever even given it a single thought." Aylia spoke firmly.

Her brother stood stone still, the truth laid bare before him. He stood up and looked at the ground. He didn't know what to do.

"Listen… Aylia, let's just calm down. Nothing needs to be decided tonight. Let's just get some rest and talk about this in the morning. We're both tired." Aylia thought of saying something else, but stopped and nodded. "You're right, Koim. Let's get some sleep."

With that they both lay down. Uncertain of what had occurred between the man and his sister, Koim drifted off into a weary sleep.

Aylia was dreaming. She stood alone on the beach looking out at the Sea. It was dusk and she watched the sunset in the distance as the sky was turning a midnight blue. She began to swim out into the open water. The sun still shone upon the water and she could see beneath her a large dark mass rising up toward her out of the depths. The absence of fear surprised her, for she was terrified of the great sharks that lived in the water. But she looked into the water with interest and joy as one of the great whales came up underneath her. Aylia floated in the water as its large nose surfaced before her and many feet behind it spray flew out of its blowhole. It did not speak with words, but its presence was motherly and comforting and Aylia understood that it wanted to show her something. So she climbed onto the large nose and sat down as the immense animal turned and carried her out toward the glowing horizon.

The whale swam out into the pink waters of the setting sun. Aylia sat hugging her knees enraptured by the colors of the sunset without a Veil to shield the shore. The bright light in the distance was ethereal and beckoned to her. In the water she could barely see the shapes of other whales swimming along with them. It began to get darker and Aylia looked back and realized how very far they had come from the shore and she became afraid. She was beyond any distance she could swim on her own. She feared being left alone in the open water. She reached her hand down and touched the whale; it was as if her feelings passed onto the whale, her uneasiness and desire to go back to the shore. Instantly the whale turned around, not because it was necessary, but because it did not want her to fear. As they traveled back to the shore, it grew darker still and Aylia fell asleep gazing at the little white barnacles that were on the whale's snout.

Aylia awoke with great turmoil in her heart, yet her fears had been calmed by her dream. It was up to her. She sat up and looked around. Koim lay sleeping on the floor with his back to her. She clutched at her heart, a great desperation filling her for she felt sure Koim would not be able to understand. She knew she lacked the ability to explain the many layers of understanding that were now flooding her heart. She rose quietly and carefully, so as not to disturb her brother's slumber.

Owls fly on silent wings
Wisdom comes to hearts that sing

No one knows the day or hour
When a bud will burst and flower

9

Japha let her hand trail across the smooth white bark of the tree as she walked by it. Ambling under the towering pine trees and swaying birch, she ran her fingers through the leaves of the undergrowth. Looking up through the windows of the forest she smiled at the holes of light that broke the fluttering canopy above her. As the wind rustled the leaves of the trees, the light seemed to dance upon her face. It was a warm afternoon. The breeze swirled around her wrapping her body in a warm hug. Turning her head at the sound of a stag alarmed by her presence, she watched him crash off through the brush. With her head turned the mark on her neck was made visible; she flinched as she lifted her hand up to the brand. The dark pink scar tissue was still tight and sudden turns of her head in the wrong direction were uncomfortable. For just a moment a solemn expression fell upon her. She shook it off and lifted her face. Not now, no sad thoughts here, she told herself. This place, these woods, this was her sanctuary; where she could go and get away from the troubled world.

Above her the trees swayed as the wind gave a gusty blast. Japha spun around in the moment, and everything slowed into a softer tremor of reality. In an instant she experienced every twittering leaf and bowing branch. She turned within a perfect place, out of time. The forest was alive and she witnessed a dance of glory. Light and leaf moving to the rhythm of creations breathe. She smiled as the frolic ended and she returned to the deer trail at her feet. Those who lived along the western border of the Shore country did not depend upon the sea for their livelihood. They were horsemen and craftsmen, outsiders among their own people.

Japha was born and raised in the foothills of the mountains. In the darkness of the large forest she felt safe and secure, where others felt trapped and lost. Her lone walks through the trees had become her only solace after she had been given the Sackeen mark. Japha's family had traded horses with the Sackeen Guard for generations. Her father was not dealing with things well, so she turned to solitude for solace. Japha was well enough acquainted with drunkenness to understand that the man she now resided with was but a shadow, a wisp, of who her father had been, or could be. Japha sighed and looked at the brook that was running past her through the green carpet at her feet. The water rushed and moved and flowed. Japha sat on the soft moss and let the cares of life and impending death lift off of her shoulders. And as she silenced the many whispers of her heart she began to *Hear*. She had heard them before, the Water words, but since her marking they had become very dear to her. She had never shared the things she saw or heard or felt in the woods with any one. It was a special time. She cherished these streams, and pools, much as Aylia did the Sea and its ripples. Although they were familiar with water in different attitudes, they heard its voice in a similar way. Japha understood that these streams were the veins, which brought life to the forest. Today they sang a song she had heard many times. *We go, we go, we flow, we flow. We seek the shore, His face to know, we run we sing, praise to the King!* In her mind's eye she saw the reunion of the water as it splashed into the Sea. Water rising to meet water in loving waves of exuberant embrace, like two lovers long separated meeting once again. Oh, the Sea, Japha had never seen it. She wondered if the sight of a mass of water so great would over whelm her. If in the many waves she had heard of, voices rose as they did from her tiny stream. Japha shut her eyes and let her heart join in the chorus of the ripples. The living laughter was always able to wash the fear and doubt from her mind. She felt renewed and after picking herself up, continued walking through the woods.

Passing under the limbs of a large leafy tree, Japha heard a branch creek above her. She turned looking up, expecting to see something like a raccoon in its branches. The hair on her arms and neck lifted silently off of her skin. The realization that she was not alone overwhelmed her; she was being watched. Her eyes saw nothing in the tree, but all of her other senses were telling her there was something near. The spirit within her began to leap about and a joy she could not explain filled her. The emotion was more than she could contain and she burst out in uncontrolled laughter as she felt someone draw near to her. Fear suddenly seized her and she stepped back ending her laughter with a bubbling inhalation that threatened to turn into a sob.

"You are safe, little one." A voice, soothing and melodic filled her head and peace washed over her. Japha dared to speak to someone she couldn't see, "Who's there?" Her voice sounded weak as it resonated through the now silent trees.

"Let all fear and doubt be washed from your heart and you shall See."

Later Japha would go over this moment again and again. How she had believed the words and obeyed without question. How in the presence of the one speaking to her she had, for the first time in her life, truly let go of all fear. She had closed her eyes and took a breath and then a step of faith.

She opened her eyes and she *Saw.* Standing before her was a woman in what appeared to be some kind of ornamental dress. A great glow shone all around her, as if she stood before the sun.

Japha stood silent and her companion gave her a moment to take in what was before her. The lady was short and fine boned. The color of her skin could not be determined for she was painted the purest white. Her eyes were dark brown and slanted, her strange features were brought together within a lovely oval. Japha saw that even her full lips appeared to be covered with the white substance. Her hair was like a headdress of white feathers. Slender arms lay down to her sides and it appeared as if she was wearing a white gown that moved like liquid, reflecting and absorbing light that was mingled with more white feathers. Japha perceived another similar in beauty and dress twenty feet or so behind the first.

Once the being before her was confident the girl had accepted what she Saw, she moved her right hand over her breast, close fisted and gave a slight bow to the young girl. The other moved simultaneously with the first. Japha stood in shocked silence. These expressions of Light, who were clearly beyond her in status and state of being, had just given her a type of salute. "Why did you do that?" Japha asked quizzically.

The nearer woman stood upright and gave a warm smile. *"To give respect to the Light that dwells in you."* The soft feminine voice filled Japha's head, and she realized the woman had not moved her lips.

Japha was in a state of stunned curiosity, "Who are you?"

The woman turned slightly and spoke, *"We are Shaunta, that is Spirit. I am Wisdom."* Motioning slightly toward the other who still remained aloof she continued, *"That is Understanding."* The feathered woman then held out to her fist, which was illuminated from within. *"We have come to wake you."*

Over an hour later Japha stood under the same tree. The Shaunta were bidding her farewell.

"Remember, little one, this is what you were designed to endure, but the choice is always yours. No one can make your decision for you, just as no one now can tell you of the joy that lies upon the distant shore especially for you... You know the Light, remain in the Light and the Light will remain in you." With this she twirled into the sky, a brilliant beam of fiery light that was joined by the second as they appeared to become entangled in many strands of pure gold before disappearing in a blink of blue flame.

What language can bring
The voice of the King?

A vision or dream
Who knows what it means?

In the dead of the night
Trembling at the sight

Of a day yet to come
And I know what will be done

10

Oya slid her feet out of her covers and let them rest on the cool floor. She stretched and roused her senses from sleepiness. An empty stillness filled the rooms of the house; her parents were up and about already. As she dressed she thought of her dream. For two weeks now she had been dreaming. Great vivid colorful dreams and she could not shake the deep-rooted understanding that was nagging at the pit of her stomach...that they *meant* something. Without even grabbing a bite to eat she went outside in search of her father.

Samuel was feeding the goats. "Well, look who finally decided to get up." He said it with a smile and Oya's eyes filled with love for the man who had always taken such good care of her and her mother. She leaned her arm over the fence to pet the kids. They were playful. "Dad, are dreams, well, meaningful?" Samuel was busy in his work letting down hay in small piles and began to quote almost absent-mindedly, "For the King may speak in one way, or in another, yet man does not perceive it. One may hear His voice in a dream, in a vision of the night, when deep sleep falls upon men, while slumbering on their beds, then He opens the ears of men, and seals their instruction." Oya did not reply as she thought this over. Samuel looked up at her and was caught by her serious expression, "Sorry, honey, did you mean something more specific?" Oya shook her head, "No, um, what you just said, what exactly does it mean?"

Samuel came out of the goat pen and they sat on a log. He looked up at the sky. "Well, I think it means that while our own mind and thoughts, are soul, is asleep, the ears of our heart and spirit remain awake, and that during that time, through a dream the King can speak to us, in a way and on a level we may not be able to when our logic or mortal limitations bar the way." Samuel continued, "You see, honey, in a dream, everything we think we know has to sit on the sidelines and watch." Oya spoke again, "Are all dreams from the King?" Samuel remembered answering the calls of his little girl in the middle of the night. Holding her while she trembled with fear of dark images that tormented her. He set his head as he gave a decidedly confident, "No." Then went on more casually, "Some come from our own soul, while others are imposters, meant to train us to be fearful. But it isn't hard to recognize if it's from the King. Your heart will tell you for one, you'll probably see more vibrant colors. Sometimes my dreams fill me with love, or joy, or peace. But even the ones from the king can be terrible and leave someone feeling shaken, simply because of its intensity or importance. People are emotional, and we can have very emotional responses to things from the Far shore. It's a very different kind of place." Oya looked up and gave a bit of a smile, "I think I understand." Samuel raised his eyebrows in surprise, "Then you are far wiser than I am, sweetie." Samuel said, then added, "Don't get to comfortable with what you think you understand about our King, just when you think you know something, it's sure to change." Oya spoke, "But the King is constant, never changing, immutable." Samuel got up and began to walk away, but said over his shoulder, so as to leave Oya sitting there thinking, "I never said He changed, we're the ones changing."

I am willing to go,
No fear will I show.

The Light has now come
And the Day has begun.

II

Japha's father found her going through her clothes in the gray twilight of evening. He leaned against the narrow doorframe, unable to say anything. There was no winning in this place. He held a mug in his hands, but couldn't find it in himself to bring it to his lips as he watched his daughter folding her garments. He wouldn't hold it against her if she ran off and tried for escape. He turned his head away and sighed. Japha stood upright as she noticed him standing there. He looked tired. He always looked tired. Deep within Japha's soul seas of unshed tears were held at bay. She loved her father. They had always been close. She remembered following him around the stables as a little girl. He had sat and showed her the intricate workings of the harness and fittings. He had spoken of things that had been beyond her years, such as how to tool leather and speak to the horses. But her father had made time for her, he had spoken to her, and she had been happy. She had always thought he was happy, too. It wasn't until last year, on her sixteenth summer that with eyes of a young woman rather than a child she had seen her father in the light of truth. He was a drunk and it broke her heart.

"Hi, Dad, you doing alright?" Japha looked at the mug, not her father as she spoke. His eyes fell to the mug as well. He could only nod. Things had been tense between them ever since Japha had received her mark. It had been a stormy night and Japha had discovered her father's mount in the stable soaked and shivering, with her father nowhere in sight. She had settled the horse down and stalled him. The wind had gusted in the barn doors, throwing them open with a great blast of haunting breath. The lightening had crackled and Japha realized she needed to go get her father and bring him home. She had saddled her own horse Bartain and set out through the storm to the tavern. She had found him there slumped over a table in the back corner. The bartender had given her a knowing nod when she walked in. No one said anything to her as she had helped her father up and out the door. She was a short girl, but her strength was great. Her father sat on her horse as she walked him through the wooded trail back to their farm. Japha had seen the small fire under the great tree near the barn. She recognized the saddles on the horses standing nearby. Sackeen's. She had no other option than to continue on into the house. She brought her father in and laid him on the couch. He was awake enough for her to see the shame and weariness in his face. He was beaten and tattered by the road he was on. That was when Japha was affronted by the purpose of the company of soldiers. She had been taken outside and marked and left in the rain. She had blacked out and would have lain out there all night, but Bartain had been left untied and he had come and stood near her. He had nickered and nuzzled her until she had woken up. She had climbed up his leg and leaned against his shoulder as they walked to the barn together. Bartain had stepped into his stall and munched on his hay. The soft straw on the floor caught Japha as she slipped into darkness once again. Her father had carried her inside the next morning. She awoke in his arms to see that he had received a mark from the soldiers, as well. A bloody gash over his right eye was visible, no doubt from the butt of a spear or sword.

Japha stood looking at her father now. Not wishing to remember all the pain and sadness. But the hurt and disappointment ran too deep. Her father finally asked, "So, you leaving then?" Japha dropped her hands to her side and turned her face away so he would not see how much the question had stung. She had thought about escape, but she could never, never leave her father, not of her own doing. No, she would stay with him to the end. "Uh, no. I might be gone for a while and I thought I would bring some of my old things over to the girls in the next glen. They're growing up fast, and I won't need these things anymore." Her father nodded as a tear escaped out of the far corner of his eye. He quietly walked away. Japha sighed and looked again at what she was doing. She continued and stuffed a large bag full of her things. She would take them over to the neighbors the next morning. But the smaller bag, her riding pants and leather chaps, boots, shirt and overcoat she would take out to the woods and stash tonight. She would go with the guards to the Sackeen ceremony, to keep her father from harm, but she had not yet committed herself to the thought that she would not be back. She sat quietly on the bed and touched the clothing in front of her. She picked up a small green tunic. It was brightly colored. She wondered why she had kept it so long. It was far too small for her now. She had worn as a child in the Harvest Festival. She had been a little firecracker of a rider and had ridden her pony in the games. She smiled at the memory. Good times. They were just images now; already her heart was becoming void of the memory of such childlike happiness. She placed the shirt in the bag; perhaps some other child would have such a day. Her father was asleep soon afterward in the front room. Japha knew she didn't have to step softly by him; there was little that could wake him from such a state. But she tip toed through the room anyway and slipped out the door. Into the dark forest she had walked. There was a hollow log not far from the house. The night was dark, but the stars were out. She looked up at the sky and took a deep breath. She thought she heard a footstep behind her. Japha stopped and looked around. Her eyes were adjusted well to the dark, but there was nothing to be seen. For a moment she entertained the thought that her father had woken up and was following her.

But then she heard a voice, soft and still, in her head, *"Just because you do not see wind, doesn't mean I am not there."* Japha looked around again. The words were strange. Doesn't mean *I am* not there? She wondered if she was hearing the voice of the wind, she knew of tales that spoke of the words of the water, could the wind have a voice as well, she wondered. Hearing nothing to alarm her in the wood, she decided to continue up the path. As she made the last turn in the trail her head was down watching the ground before her, being careful of her steps. She did not see the soft glow of light that was emanating from the person who was sitting on the log. His appearance was unexpected, but she didn't startle at the sight of him. There was a warmth and comfort in the air that fear could not penetrate. Japha stood alone in the dark staring at the odd looking man.

"You have come far little one, I thought it was time we had a proper introduction." Japha stood staring, and then smiled, she couldn't help herself. She could smell something in the air that was sweat. "I know you," she said, "How do I know you? You seem so familiar to me." He smiled. It was a pleasant smile. He had a pure white moustache and beard, which only allowed his lower lip to show as the corners of his mouth turned upward. He had white, pure white, skin and hair. His eyes were dark and slanted, Japha thought they looked like the deepest softest doe eyes she had ever seen, but they were intelligent, very intelligent. He wore a full-length coat that stretched to the ground like a robe. It appeared to be made out of soft tawny deerskin and it was edged with soft white fur. A large hood hung back off of his shoulders. Japha moved to put down her sack. He stood up and reached

for it. *"You don't want to leave that just lying around anywhere."* He said as he took it from her just before it touched the ground. When he moved he seemed to flicker. Japha's gaze was drawn to his hand as it reached out from the long sleeve of the coat he was wearing. His skin was white yet iridescent, with fine white hair on the back of his hand, just like all men had. But his fingernails had almost a claw like appearance to them. Not menacing, but showing of great strength.

He took the bag and walked over to place it inside the log, exactly where she had intended to put it. Her voice came out strange and squeaky. "How did you know that I ...that I was..?" He turned his head and smiled again as he finished shoving the bag out of sight. *"Because, it was my idea to put it there."* His voice sounded like a man, and yet there was a watery undercurrent of something like laughter that Japha couldn't quite pin down. She felt that she could listen to him speak forever, and more than that, it was comforting and familiar sound, because this voice *had always* comforted her. Japha stood still, unsure of what to do or say, but feeling so happy, so very happy, to be here, to be with him. He came toward her and stood. She looked into his eyes; they seemed to contain the night sky, a watery darkness that twinkled with light. "Who are you?" He gave a slight nod in acknowledgement that she needed him to explain. *"I am Three, I am Anari."*

Japha was speaking now, "So all those times, those times of warmth, and goodness that came through when I was alone, or upset, about my parents, or me, those words in my head, they weren't my own thoughts, that was you?" Anari was sitting on the ground leaning up against the log. Japha sat on a branch that curled out from the fallen tree. He propped his arm up on one knee as he spoke. *"They were my Father's words, but it was my voice you heard. From across the Sea my Father watches all of his children. And he is especially fond of you. The turmoil you went through over your mother and father could have been a great setback for you. But you have been chosen to be here at the end of the old and the beginning of the new. So he sent you words of encouragement, and gave you instruction so that you would not fail.*" He sat up and turned toward her. She watched him, it was beautiful when he moved, the light that came from him wavered and he was hard to see. Like a when water is troubled and the reflection is lost until the ripples cease. "*There was a time when you considered leaving your father, when it became so hard for you to see him and what he did. We spoke to you and told you that the kind of daughter you were to be did not depend on the type of father you had.*" Japha looked at the ground. The words were true, but she was ashamed that she had ever thought of writing her father off. "*There now, don't be ashamed, the thought of leaving was completely natural for your survival, you were dealing with things that were very hard to bear. And just as you should not feel bad about desiring to leave, so you should not give yourself too much credit for staying. You were in no physical danger, yet your heart was being broken day after day. We simply gave you the strength to endure it. This was the will of my Father and it was our voice that comforted and instructed you.*" Japha considered all this.

They sat in silence for a time and then Anari looked up at the night sky. "*It's nearly time.*" The phrase hung in the air and Japha looked at him, struck by the serious expression that was on his face now. He looked almost fierce, a white lion of a man. He stood and picked up a long staff that had been leaning against the dead tree. Japha stood up as well. When he turned around he was shining a bit more brightly than he had been before. "*Japha, there is a task that needs to be done. Just as you have stayed true to your father here, the one across the shore is asking you to be true to him even though it may cost you your life.*" Japha nodded. The Shaunta had spoken to her of the sacrifice and of the decision before her. "*Don't be afraid, my brother will be there with you.*

Remember, you are never alone, even if you can't see me, I am always with you." He then reached into his covering and pulled from his chest what appeared to be a heavenly light, a tiny ball of white that was fringed in blue. He took her hand and placed it in her palm and then pressed her hand upon her chest. A wave of light and love ***Boomed*** within her and she was shaken and found herself amongst the pile of clothes on her bed.

Warriors bound
 In darkness keep,
 Men of power
 Plot and seek
  The less will rise
   Their hope to claim
  The great will fall
 To pits of shame.

12

Lord Faxim was giving only half of his attention to the ramblings of his chief advisor as he gazed out of an open window. The city of Ohim, capital of the Shore, was the jewel in his crown. The desk was littered with papers and books. He was deep in thought and was fidgeting with the gold rings on his fingers absentmindedly. His advisor grew bolder in his speech, "My Lord, think of the advantage we could have if we could harness and turn these *gifts*. The possibilities are endless." Faxim was growing tired of these arguments. He turned, "No. It is not worth the risk." His hands shuffled through the pages on the table as he continued, "I've spent extensive time reading the records of the Sea Folk. Such ambitions became the downfall of every nation that has ruled over them. The temptation to use them or wipe them out has brought about the destruction of many." Faxim sighed; he had contemplated the decision for a long time. "No, we will simply continue to diminish the threat through sacrifice." He turned back toward the window. He had no way of knowing if his decision would prove to be effective in years to come. The Sea Folk as a people were as turbulent and unsettled as the Sea itself. Ruling them was a political nightmare, but it was a price Faxim was willing to pay to be in control of the Shore.

He began to speak, as if he was unaware that there were still others in the room. "In my dreams the Sea calls to me with a voice that stirs my very soul with a longing to see the mysteries of the deep. Yet, I come here and find a strange people, a nation of sleeping giants. We seek to control them in vain, in a vision of the night I saw, I have heard the great call of a trumpet that rouses them from their slumber. Oh, what a terrible day that will be, the streets will be filled with blood and we will suffer greatly for what we have done." His voice trailed off as his eyes were held by the sight of the distant waves that glittered in the sun beyond the rooftops. His counselors glanced at each other, unsure of the meaning of their Lord's words. "Such a day," he turned back toward the men, his chin near his chest, "such a day I do not wish to see." He stood up and spoke decidedly, "No, I will keep them asleep as long as possible. The marked ones are to die."

Dark and dank; the caverns of the Dragons were bustling with activity. All through the night the riders slept while their pages worked and hauled and tended the dragons. They needed to be fed lightly tonight. The riders had already bathed and scrubbed their beasts and now slept as their slaves finished the preparations for the morning assignment. Unnoticed and despised, many pages longed for a simple snort of disgust from the great beasts. The stone hollow of the empty mountain was cold under the vast night sky. Torches lit the way of the drudges and fires burned to keep the cold serpents warm in the caves. A page drudged on, trying to keep his mind on his work. Akail was tall and lanky, nearly eighteen he was a quiet and gentle slave. Although the dragons were awe inspiring to watch in flight, he did not enjoy life in the Keep. He worked long into the night cleaning his master's armor. The call for the Gathering had come late in the day. Akail was sore and tired as the first glimpse of light began to threaten to overcome the high peaks. He walked into a small room and placed a large sword in the corner of the room. It was finely polished and he had restrung the red threading through the belt. His master, a rider named Kaxil, used red to accent every piece of his rigging and clothing to compliment his mount. His dragon Farn was a black dragon, with just the slightest points of red that glistened when he was in the light.

Akail was tired and wiped a smudge of black dirt from his face. He turned and looked out the small opening into the lair of the dragons. This place looked like hell, and to Akail it was. No grass or trees, only an open bowl of black rock that was unbearably hot during the day and cold as ice at night. He hoped one day to escape, but not today. He stood with one hand on the rock face, his head tilted ever so slightly as he let himself dream of another life, of his mother and family. His brown hair hung down over his forehead. His blue eyes pierced the many shades of gray that surrounded him. Color was rare within the Keep. Even the sleek bodies of the dragons were earth tones of brown, pale green, gray and black. A slight smile crossed his face as he remembered being young and running through fields of green tipped with flowers of many colors.

His daydreaming came to a sudden halt as Kaxil spun him around without warning. He held the boy by his shirt; Akail leaned back as his balance was held by his master. "It's nearly dawn, boy! Why didn't you wake me?" Akail stuttered and stammered trying to bring his thoughts back to this reality. "I…I was just about to, sir." His voice was a squeak. Kaxil smiled at him. "Well, what are you waiting for?" He asked as he pushed the Akail through the doorway, "Go get my breakfast!" Akail turned quickly once he was released. Kaxil never hurt him, the rider's tone made Akail wonder if his master was stressed about this morning's business. The sound of his footsteps was lost amongst the many sounds of dragons and riders as they awoke and began to prepare for the Gathering.

The Temple walls were no longer over laid with gold. The pillars of cedar were showing age. Fine linens that hung as great curtains were dusty and faded. None of the beautiful adornments that once filled the Temple of the Sea Folk had been overlooked when the Sackeens had conquered and pillaged. The building however was still a sacred place. The last tribute left that told of the wealth and power that had once belonged to these people. The days of favor from across the Sea now seemed lost. Those who ruled and taught in the temple did so in honor of their way of life and traditions. Although they honored the King with their way of life, their hearts were far from him. Voices filled the main sanctuary as many men had argued into the night. The religious leaders walked a dangerous line. They lived in between two very different ways of life. The priests tried to gain power and wealth from both sides. To their own people they portrayed a protective line of tradition and politics as they dealt with the Sackeen governors. To the Sackeen's they were agreeable for the right price. The Temple leaders controlled the mob of the people and so they used their advantage of knowledge and position to exploit their fellow countrymen whenever they could. They were not all corrupt, but it was not easy to walk according to the traditions of a culture that was so radically different than those who had conquered it. Compromise was bound to happen in one form or another. Tonight voices were angry and the conversation heated as the Temple leaders discussed the fabled 'wizard' of the Sea Folk.

This Barduuk had become a serious problem. The wonders he performed had made him extremely popular among the people. There were many who now spoke openly that he was perhaps the son of the King across the Sea. Come to free the Sea Folk of the Sackeen's. But his teachings and interpretation of the writings many times contradicted the customs they had followed for centuries now. Instead of feeling hope in the promise of a new king, many of the Priests felt threatened. He had to be dealt with. They argued now over just how it would be done. Some of the men wished to make a public spectacle of him, while others thought it wiser to murder him quietly. "If you kill him publicly you risk open riots!" one shouted, his face red behind his gray beard. Another countered, "An open trial, in front of the people would expose him and his black arts, much of the damage he has done would be repealed." Still another shouted out in fear and rage, "I will not risk my life on such a hope, who knows how the mob will react and we may be the ones who are put on trial!" They all began to shout at once until Dalub, the Elder of the Sea called for order. He was short and hunched over in age, but his eyes were still sharp and he spoke with the weight of his years behind him. "Why do we not now consider a way in which the Sackeen's can yet be of use? They are learned in our ways and fearful of our prophecies; let us use that to our advantage." The idea had merit. The shouting ceased and low murmuring began as they plotted to do just as Dalub had suggested.

Keys to lock and bars to hold.
A mystery is found and told

Of love and loss,
And pain for gain,
Into the dark,
His right to claim.

13

Alone on the dark shoreline Barduuk knelt in the cool sand. His pants were wet from the seawater that cascaded upon him again and again as he listened. He needed comfort tonight. The light from the moon gave a faint glow to his face and the water before him, but he felt no warmth from it. He lowered his eyes and cried. Great tears burst forth. He sobbed and trembled. The Sea gently lapped against his knees and thighs again and again. A cool wet comfort spoke, *"We are here, we are here, do not fear, the end is near."* Barduuk sobbed again, he brought his hands to his face. He had done everything he could. He allowed himself to be a conduit to bring the light to this shore. But these little ones were not ready for such light. He knew they would be coming for him very soon, and he was afraid. His sobs subsided and he let his arms fall to his side. Soft gray bubbles in the ripples around him spun and twirled with the motion of the waves. The round spheres clung to his pants and would not let go until they were broken by the next wave that crashed into them. Barduuk lifted his eyes, neither would he let go of this shore. Not until the next wave, the new beginning had come. Not until they realized what was possible.

Out into the sea a large wave stretched out from the north to the south as far as he could see. He watched as it rose like great white heads of many lions, the spray lifting as wide wings from their backs. The water called out in a mighty roar as it reflected what it had seen on the other shore, an army, ready and waiting to come to the call of their Prince, if he so desired. The thought gave him strength. He spoke and the water grew still as it listened, "I will be with you soon, Father, and I will not return empty handed." Barduuk braced himself as he felt someone draw near. No footsteps were heard pressing into the sand as Ophinum came toward the man on his knees. The Liar hunched down low and eyed the man. His voice was sweet, "You cannot win the hearts of men. After your flesh ends, the next generation will forget you, why do you contend for those who are content to remain in the dark?" Suddenly Barduuk's body lurched and his back arched. Agony enveloped him. A blade of green blackness protruded out of his chest. His oppressor had stabbed him in the back with his sword. The blade did not pierce flesh, but spirit, it was drenched in fear that spread like poison through the soul of the man. Next to his ear Ophinum opened his mouth and whispered, "Now" he paused as he relished Barduuk's agony, "... now you know, the full extent of fear. You have come so far for them. They would not do the same for you, *they* would not risk so much!" A foamy substance was splattered on Barduuk's face from the lips that had spoken. The slimy specks moved like spiders and crawled beneath the flesh. Droplets of blood leaked out across his face. The man trembled in terror that ultimately separated him from all other memory or emotion. He felt completely alone. "Father, help me." He called out to the other shore, a coast he could no longer see. He asked for help from someone, whose voice he could not hear, through the fear that pounded like drumbeats through his being. The green veins of moving vapor continued to spread through him. His hands shook unable to even move to his chest, the greatest point of pain.

Barduuk dipped his head and forced himself to remember. Remember, an afternoon with his father, walking along that opposite shore. It took every drop of self-control he could muster to call into focus one memory. He remembered the words of his Father, and why he had come. At that instant a light exploded from his chest and the black dagger was thrown from his body. A shockwave extended out in all directions from the spot and his oppressor was gone. Barduuk lay on his back as a small wave crashed into him and he opened his eyes and saw light. Two great glowing forms were standing over him. Something was put to his lips and he was told to drink. He drank what seemed like hot honey. Warmth spread over him as if the substance was unrolled within him like a scroll. He lay on the sand until he was completely restored and breathing easily. A few minutes later he stood and saw his helpers vanish, and in the space where they once stood he saw a strand of torchlight moving up the shoreline.

The Keys clinked and jingled against the rod they hung from. The staff rose and fell as the one who carried it moved through the darkness to a round doorway that lay flat as if it was a table. Deep within the earth, roots and rock were woven together with the purest gold. The frame was encased with a layer of diamond like substance, which cast flickers of light in many hues. A great lock covered the front of the portal. Many layers of what looked like a mechanical wheel within a wheel wound around a lock. The ancient and intricate key was placed in the hole that was made for it. A gasp was heard as the mechanism turned and opened revealing a liquid surface that rose and stretched as it awoke. A substance, which displayed the attributes of fire and water, quivered within the open chasm. The Lie lowered his lips and spoke a single word. It was spoken with hate, with envy, and disgust and the name hovered as a low hiss until it fell and was absorbed by the trembling entity. *"Barduuk."* A strange fluid form rose from the open portal, it heaved as if it took in a deep breath and then released a deafening cry. Moving upward it swelled as it rose through the darkness. The chasms within the black heart of the world shook as the voices of thousands upon thousands joined in Death's toll.

If I could take you far away,
 Would you go or would you stay?

Together in the darkness bare,
 My children sit, so young so fair.

 Your time has come,
 You now can See,
More than you, shall be set free.

The clouds will part, the dawn will break,
All I do is for your sake.

No longer then shall we foresee
But in the Light, forever be.

14

Akail handed the dragon rider his provisions then watched as regiment dragons achieved the sky. As the strong wind from the downbeat of the dragon's wings died down Akail remained with his face uplifted toward the steely expanse. The slender page watched as the Riders went to collect the marked Seafarers. His hands did not move from his side as droplet after droplet of water tumbled out of his eyes. He felt the tiny wet fingers of his tears cascade down his face like wavelets. He wished they could wipe away his sorrow, and cleanse him of his part in this day of death. He tried to picture the faces of the marked, but he didn't even know their names. He tried to picture other children, like himself, but it had been many seasons since he had seen one. Akail finally lowered his eyes from the bright morning to the dark cavernous walls of the Keep. He was a prisoner here. Although he cared for the dragon rider he served, he found no joy here. For within the shell of the thin dirty boy in rags, beat the young heart of a true-born Sea Farer. The mystery of what lay on the other side of that seemingly endless body of water was hid in heart, like a thorn in his palm. Buried deep within his flesh, he was unable to free himself of the hope he had of something more; of a day, far off, but coming none-the-less. When he would see Light, and once again feel the spray of sea on his face. He returned a few discarded items back to his master's room.

Akail's dirty hands gently touched the leather of books and other items left disheveled across the dressing table. He had a good master. A tinge of lost hope and regret panged in the boy's chest as he thought of the first day he had met Kaxil. Akail had been only eight years old when he was brought to the Keep to serve as slave and servant to the dragon riders. Shy and reserved he wouldn't speak, and had been the smallest of the group. One of the older dragon riders had taken to roughing him up in an attempt to get him to say his name. Dragon riders were traditionally good to their slaves. There was little chance of escape from the Keep as dragons were the only way in or out. Yet, on occasion as in any other arena, the men of the Keep could be cruel and heartless. The bright red of Kaxil's jacket had drawn Akail's attention to the young man who seemed to flinch and look away when the grizzly dragon rider had knocked the small boy over. Yet, Kaxil hadn't been able to walk away. Akail had watched the tall rider stride over, placing a hand on Tarken's arm, staying the next blow. "If you don't mind, I'd like to claim him while he's still in one piece." Kaxil had spoken lightly, not wanting to draw attention to what he was doing. Tarken eyed Kaxil; he didn't like being denied his sport. He had glanced back at the boy then to Kaxil. He didn't know the young rider well, but Kaxil was respected for his ability in the games and a favorite to become a wing leader. "You'll need to bottle feed this one boy." Tarken sneered as he let the young Akail flop to the floor. Akail remembered the look on the elder riders face as he walked away. He still feared that man, not only for himself but for his master as well. Somehow on that day, Kaxil and Akail came to an unspoken understanding of acceptance for each other. Although it never blossomed into friendship a bond was set in place by an unseen third party.

Akail sighed as the darkness of the Keep threatened to swallow him yet again. Pulling the skin curtain back he stepped out of the hollow. His thin frame seemed to crumple into a small round corner in the stone near Kaxil's lair. He gently pulled on the strand around his neck and revealed a small leather pouch. He turned it over in his hand and let a small blue stone plop out onto his palm. It was the only thing he had been able to hold onto throughout the years, a token of home. The trinket was from another time, his memory of another place. The world around him faded way into the sunlight and the warmth of that day. His mother had placed the bright stone in his hand and covered it with hers. "It's yours, my son. Just like your name or face. The color blue rests on you. It is the color of the secrets, the secrets of the Other shore." Akail had looked with wide eyes at the small stone. They had walked and talked of many things. Of how the surface of the water reflected the world above, but within the depths the water held mysteries. "That's because the king has hidden his secrets there." She said as she squatted down next to him and leaned over the edge of the rock they sat on. Her head had tilted to one side as if listening to the gentle pool that swirled and splashed against the stone. "And if you learn to listen, and quiet waves of your own heart, the water will speak to you." Akail had looked into the water doubtingly and then back at his mother. "What will it say?" He asked. Lifting her head she had laughed at the serious look on his childish face. "No one can tell you that, honey. But some say that within the deep blue depths, the water carries the words of the great king himself who lives on the other side of the sea." He remembered looking down at the shimmering surface and seeing his reflection encompassed by the blue sky that was mirrored with him. The day had been full of hugs and laughter. They had splashed in the water then bathed in the sunlight. Akail put the stone away and leaned against the bleak jagged rock as his side. He was tired. Heavy eyelids drooped as sleep over came him and he dreamt. He dreamt of someone, with a voice like his mothers, bidding him up. And he flew up, high into the sky. He flew past the dragons and darkness, flew out over the rolling sea, toward a growing light behind a dark horizon.

Aylia had spent two nights in her own bed. Her parents were bound by grief, yet they had been given a peace and were trying to cope. They were all anxious for Koim and hoped he would follow Aylia home soon. The three of them spent much time together, talking, laughing and crying together. This morning Aylia sat up in bed and thought she was still dreaming as she became aware of a man, clothed in golden light, standing in the doorway. He had great wings that were illuminated. His head was bowed so that she could not see his face. The room was filled with a sweet smell and a peace fell over her. She relaxed and felt sleepy as he raised his head just enough to give her a quick knowing smile. "It will be alright, little one. We are with you." With that he began to fade from view. The entire house then trembled as it was accosted by great gusts of wind. As she pulled her feet out her blankets, the armored figure of a dragon rider burst through the golden dust that still hung in the doorway.

Kaxil grabbed Aylia without word and examined her mark. She went numb and dumb, unable to speak as he pulled her out of the house. Tabor sprang out of the door, his paternal instincts to protect her spilling over. The large face of the dragon appeared over them, giving a low growl that made even the dirt and rocks tremble. The rider turned and looked at the parents of his charge with surprise, waiting until they realized that they would not be contending against a man alone, but a battle tested dragon. Tabor raised his hands and lowered his head in submission. Rapha lunged onto her daughter and hugged her fiercely. In her ear she whispered, "My beautiful girl!" Aylia touched her mother's hair one last time gently and quietly, not in grief but in love.

Kaxil wrenched the girl from her mother's grasp, irritated by the scene. He pushed her toward the winged serpent. Aylia was unable to move as the dragon opened its wings and shaded her from the light of the sun. The dragon, whose name was Farn, quivered as Kaxil lifted the slender passenger onto his neck. The feeling was mutual; Aylia cringed at the sensation of the scaly skin beneath her. She looked down at her parents as they stood in the shadow of the dragon. Kaxil climbed into the saddle behind her and wrapped a strong arm around her. The frailty of her form in his embrace caused a wave of tender paternal mercy to wash over him that he had not been prepared for. The windblown sent of sea grass filled his head as her hair was blown in his face. He turned his countenance away from the long strands as his dragon lunged into the air with great force. In that moment Aylia was thankful for the strength of the rider as he held her fast. Once in the air Aylia leaned back into his arms. Somehow, she knew that this man would not let her fall.

The wind was cold and she wore only her thin nightgown. Kaxil felt her shiver and was confused by the pity he felt for her. Farn was uneasy and flying evasively. Kaxil looked behind him, and saw nothing but open sky. *Calm down, big boy. She's seems tame enough.* He tried to relax, so as to impart calmness to Farn, yet he was upset himself. Ripping children from their mother's arms was not what he considered a soldier's duty. He could feel the tension growing in his partner. Farn imparted back to Kaxil, *the light is bright and strange.* Kaxil wasn't sure he understood, but Farn would not discuss it now. Riders were told that dragons could perceive things that were invisible to men. But dragons gave up long ago trying to explain the world as they saw it, in truth many dragons wondered how men got around at all with such a limited sight.

Farn beat his wings, increasing his velocity, desiring to be rid of his charge. But the stone courtyard, in Ohim, was no relief. It was not that the Light caused dragons pain, but it disoriented them for they were not accustomed to it. At least five other dragons had already set down their collections and the place was full of glowing figures. Farn arched his neck and buried his head beneath his foreleg. Farn's behavior was unusual. Kaxil surveyed the yard and noticed the disturbed behavior of the other dragons and shrugged. *It must be a dragon thing*, he thought.

Dismounting, he pulled Aylia off Farn's neck. She was faint and practically fell into his arms. A gentle shake helped her back to her senses. "Are you alright?" he asked quietly. Aylia got her feet under her grabbing his arms to steady her. She looked up at him and nodded. Kaxil noticed her face; it seemed to glow as the image was burned into his being. He became aware of every line, every slope of her features, and the wreath of earthy brown and gold that framed the soft skin. Her eyes were, so large and deep, as if they contained the depth of the sea itself. Within a child he *Saw* the light of world. Kaxil was fixed in the moment, unable to move as this picture of Aylia was traced onto the canvas of his mind. Aylia tilted her head, unsure of what had come over him. She saw an image of large golden hands resting over his eyes. She watched as the hands were raised and Kaxil blinked and cleared his throat as he shuffled his feet, letting go of her. Aylia stood before him, her tiny hands on his arms. Looking at him, somehow she knew that he was not lost, although now he stood before her dressed as her enemy. She knew that one day; he would awaken out of darkness. A love like the one she had for Koim was stirred and a sweet smile was exchanged between the two of them.

Padded feet shuffled across the paved stone and brought the moment to an end. The shaved head of the eunuch was bowed in reverence to the dragon and its master. The length of his robe was draped across his forearm and in his hand he held a chain. As he approached he gave a slight salute to Kaxil. Kaxil's eyes fell to the bonds he carried. Without thinking Kaxil took Aylia by the shoulder protectively. He couldn't collect his thoughts. He had a duty, but felt a natural need to guard this strange sea fairy of a girl. Aylia felt the pressure of his hand on her arm and looked up. His manner was so similar to Koim's; the same confused but protective expression was on his face. She spoke as she moved lightly out of his grasp, "I'll be all right. I'm ready to go now." Kaxil looked at her, unable to make sense of what was happening. He stepped back as the eunuch bound Aylia's wrists and led her away in chains. Farn was trembling and Kaxil turned his attention to his dragon. Once Kaxil was back in the saddle Farn raised his head. His dragon eyes saw small and intense points of light walking around like men. Farn was aware that the Light was affecting his rider as well, but could tell it was not harmful and so did not mention it. Kaxil tried to push the girl from his mind as he asked Farn to take to the air. Aylia watched as they rose into a canopy of blue sky.

Japha was alone, carrying her bundle of clothes through the woods to her neighbor's house. The trees around her had creaked and moaned. Japha fell back on her rump as an immense brown dragon landed in a small clearing just before her. She stood up, leaving the bundle where it had fallen. A tall barrel chested man hopped off the dragon and eyed her suspiciously. She was dressed for walking in the forest; faded green leggings and knee-high leather boots. Her tunic was simple but heavy enough to keep her warm in the shade of the trees. The rider's eyes fell to the bundle she had dropped and he suspected her of trying to flee from her fate. He hunched as he pulled a small knife from his belt. "Well, now girly, you going on a little trip? Looky you," He chuckled. "I thought we were out to gather a daughter of the sea today, not a wood nymph. Are you fixing to give Braken and me a little sport this morning?" Japha glanced at the bag near her feet. She closed her eyes and took in a deep breath. She did not waver in the moment, the place where her decision had to become her actions. Her gaze leveled on the man as he smiled at the thought of hunting her through the brush. She knew he would suffer consequences if she were harmed. The dragon caught her attention. She had never seen one so close before. Her spine straightened with the realization that one of the terrors of her people was about to suffer her upon its back. Lifting her leg she took a very determined step over her bag and strode toward the brown beast. The rider lowered his knife and looked at her in awe as she paraded past him like a queen. Her chin held high so he could clearly see the mark she bore. Unable to account for the girl's behavior, Tarken sheathed his knife and walked disappointedly after her.

The dragon, Braken, began to shift uneasily as the young woman drew near. He seemed to want to back away from her. Tarken was unable to calm him down. His talons tore up the forest floor and his tail lashed about like a twenty-foot whip. The bumbling dragon rider tried in vain to calm his friend. He thanked the gods that none of his associates were around to see as his 'prisoner' sat on a rock, placing her chin in her hands as he tried to calm his beast. Japha finally became tired of waiting, and standing up, spoke to the dragon herself. "I don't like this any more than you do, but calm down now and *BE STILL.* You'll be in trouble if you're flailing around causes me harm." The large brute instantly stood still. Braken, his eyes closed, did not move as Japha stepped up to him and took hold of the harness. Tarken ran up and grabbed her hand as she prepared to pull herself up. She stopped and looked at him. Shaking his head in disbelief he stated, "A nymph ya must be if even my own dragon will obey you!" Japha just looked at him. She simply shrugged as she swung herself up. He glanced at Braken and shook his head in disbelief. He had not expected any of this.

Japha grew somber and tears flowed as she looked down at the forest from the sky. She felt naked and alone in the open sky outside of the comforting closeness of the trees. She saw the roof of her house in the distance. Now her father would be completely alone. The reality hit her hard in the stomach. She looked back as she heard the faint call of her horse, "It's okay, Bartain," she whispered into the wind, "you take care of Daddy now."

In the barn near the edge of the trees Bartain began to pound heavily on the stall door with his hoof. Gerdon, up and nearly sober, let his bucket down and walked over to try to sooth Japha's horse. Bartain would not be quieted, but changed tactics and began peeling out long cries and craning his neck over the side of his stall toward the open door. Gerdon walked over and raised his arm to shield his eyes from the glare of the morning. He could just make out the shape of a dragon rising above the trees, and he realized Japha was being taken. His arm dropped as he crumpled to the ground. The deafening cries of the horse over and over again paralleled the shattering of Gerdon's heart. *Neigggghhhhh, Pound.* The barn rattled. *Crack, Tang, crash,* a layer of self-preservation broke and fell, Gerdon shook. *Neigggghhhh.*

Pound. The stall door was cracked. *Crack, tang, crash.* The shattering sound of breaking glass resonated within the confines of the human soul. Gerdon wept, as layer upon layer walls were broken. There was nothing else to hold onto, nothing to keep him from completely letting go. He fell, deep into the heartaches that he had managed to detain for years by keeping a mug to his lips.

Beat your wings, you flying fate
I will stand and I will wait.

Your strength and might is all in vain
He has come to take our pain.

The Word rings true,
The Word cuts deep
So fly away, back to your Keep.

I cannot keep what is not mine
For darkness proceeds what is divine.

15

Samuels's eyes were stern and unflinching as the first rays of morning light shone on him. His face was streaked with tears, but his expression was one of grim determination. He sat on the rock again in front of his house. His song, bittersweet, rose into the air. A dragon was circling high overhead, and had been for nearly twenty minutes now. Samuel had come out while it was still dark and thought to sing hello to the dawn. Night had come to him instead. He knew why the flying fear had come. He had raised his voice higher as it had approached. It had spun in the air when it intersected with his song. A song of radiance of the far shore had stopped the dragon in midair. Samuel had paused in his tune for just an instant when he realized what had happened. He redoubled his voice and sang out all the more. He knew he couldn't sing forever, his voice would eventually give out. But he would not let his daughter go without making some sort of stand. He was not a man of battle or armor. The bard had not yet come to understand that music superseded the mortal realm and flowed like strong waves in the unseen world around him. These waves were crashing against the dragon when he dared to land near. Samuel kept on singing, trying to usher in hope. Lifting his heart along with his voice and hoping for some kind of salvation to come.

The dragon was tiring from the battle with the light song and he let out a pitiful cry. Samuel's eyes darted to the corner of his face when he heard Oya and her mother come out the door.

Oya looked up and *Saw* waves of gold and orange swirling in the air above. She looked back to her father. Such tender love, her heart went out to him. She knew it was not easy for him to say good-bye. Her mother covered her mouth and began to sob. She reached out to Oya with both hands and Oya held her one last time. But then she pulled her mother off of her and turned and walked toward source of the flow. Samuel felt his daughter's hand on his shoulder. He shook his head and continued playing. Not yet, he wasn't ready. She finally reached around him and placed her hand, gently but firmly upon the strings of his instrument. Placing her hands on his cheeks, she looked into his eyes. Around the corners of those lovely windows, she saw the marks of many smiles. How she longed to see him smile right now. "Daddy, I need you to say good-bye." Samuel slumped forward, his arms hanging around his strings. He breathed in a heavy broken breath and looked at his child. He reached out and touched her face. "You are so beautiful." More tears ran out of him. With that he dropped his hand and set his eyes on the featherless green wings that were now landing nearby. Oya turned and walked toward the rider as he slipped of his mount. She looked at her mama one more time and mouthed, *I love you.* Samuel let his head drop again, in final submission to the fate that had fallen on his house. Oya prepared herself to be lifted onto the dragon, but the rider strode angrily past her without even a word. Before he realized what had happened, Samuel was pulled off the rock and punched squarely in the mouth, knocking Samuel over. Blood covered his lips and he spat and sputtered as he brought a hand to his lips. The dragon rider then turned on his strings and bashed it to pieces against the boulder. Harmony was shattered and the discord of broken wood and strings filled the air. Samuel sat up, gently touching his lip with the back of his hand as he watched the rider do his work. When the Sackeen had finished, he turned expecting Samuel to retaliate. Samuel simply spit blood on the ground and turned his eyes to Oya. He could make another guitar. His eyes contorted in agony, he could never make another Oya. The rider followed the man's gaze to his daughter and looked back as Samuel with interest and understanding. He grumbled and kicked dust at him, but seeing that there was no more fight left in him; he walked back to Oya and pushed her up onto his dragon. Oya's last glimpse of her father was of him burying his face into her mother's breast as she knelt and embraced him.

Oya's ride to the Sackeen temple city was short and her rider silent. He did not even dismount when they landed. He simply flung her off of his beloved animal onto the hard ground. She landed on her hands and knees in a cloud of dust. Brushing herself off, she stood up, and let herself be bound and led to the prison below.

Oya was taken to a small stone corridor. Lined up upon the wall were nearly a dozen young Sea folk, boys and girls. Oya didn't recognize anyone, and yet felt deeply interested in who they were.

Stepping out from the blackness at the end of the hall was a figure, cloaked in red from head to toe. It stepped toward Oya slowly. The Swayking, the leader of the Searchers, examined her. Oya lost her breath at the sight of his eyes. They were yellow ringed in orange light and bore through her very being. And then around his brow he wore an odd crown. Oya gasped as he stepped closer and she saw that the crown was a living creature, wrapped around his head in such a way that it's one large eye rested in the middle of his forehead. Although he gazed at Oya with a hollow penetrating gaze, he spoke to another cloaked figure, unnoticed in the corner, "She is the last?" He spoke with a deep voice that held many undercurrents that seemed to float in the air around the words he had spoken. The brown hood nodded in silence. He looked Oya over; these youths were oddities no doubt. Being now satisfied that they were all accounted for he instructed that they be made ready. Oya was pressed into the group. She tried to search their faces, but the light was dim and soon they were being led through another hallway. As they were shuffling through the stone ways, Oya felt a small warm hand press into hers. She grasped it and tried not to cry out loud. Aylia gave her a slight squeeze of reassurance. Without a word spoken the two of them became the dearest and closest of friends as they walked together into the depths.

Awake, my son
Let go of shame
Arise, my son
To hear your name
You now have lost
What you tried to hold
If you will listen,
You will be told.

16

Koim looked out over the glassy Sea. The sun was bright this morning. His back was turned away from the other men on the boat. He had been standing at the bow since midnight. He had waited for the dawn, seething in anger and despair. Daring the sun to rise and greet him when all he was had grown cold. His hands gripped the rail before him. He gazed out upon the water as the golden rays attempted to warm him. He ignored them. The ship rose and fell and the Sea tried to get his attention. Flicking up long thin fingered of water droplets that tickled his face. His warm tears melted away the cool touch of the spray. *How could she go back?* He thought to himself. *I never should have let her out of my sight!* He'd been severe upon himself, blaming his own lack of protection for her escape. He had tried to pursue her that first morning. Climbing up the first hill out of Navar, he had looked as far as his sharp eyes could see. There was nothing to be seen. She was at least a full ten hours ahead of him. Aylia was agile and spry he doubted he would catch up to her. He knew where she had gone, and why. He understood, but he did not share her feelings. This was suicide. He had fallen to his knees and cried out in despair. He had mourned for his baby sister, who he loved so dearly. He had looked up into the sky, hands full of dirt and grass he had lifted his fists up and squeezed until his palms gave way to the tiny rocks concealed within the earth and bled. "Why!!" He had shouted to the heavens. The image of the man, the man walking in the rain had flooded his mind. The words of the old man in the eatery resurfaced, "He's a Sea Farer too. That I would live to see one of our people turn to the dark forces." Koim was a simple but proper Sea Farer, he had kept with all of their customs and rules his entire life, without blemish. He knew he would be no match against a wizard; he had no knowledge of how to undo a curse. He had wandered back to the loft and gathered his things. He would go north up the shore. To the Tower, to the school of the priests and he would learn of the ancient ways, of how evil was undone. With every wave that brought him closer to the Tower, his resolve became firmer. When he achieved his destination he would write to his parents and inform them of his plans.

His eyes fell down to the moving water as the ship rose and crashed into to, splitting the sea before it, forcing the swells to give way. He heard no words, he hoped for none. His mind was filled with a call to arms against the one who had bewitched his sister. He looked up toward the Veil that hung out in the distance concealing the mysteries that lay beyond. He knew there was a king out there, but for now he also knew that such a king had not showed up when his sister, along with so many others, had needed him the most. No. The King had left such a charge to men, the men of the Shore, to be strong, to take care of their people, to guard them from the influence of the Sackeen's and any other corruption that might come. With anger in his heart, he set out to become powerful, terribly powerful.

A bucket clanked against a feeding bin. The familiar nicker of a horse beckoned to someone it knew. Gerdon rolled over on the floor of the barn. The day was passing overhead. He lifted his hand and rubbed his face. *How long have I been asleep?* He wondered. "Oh, about eight hours now, I'd say." Gerdon tilted his head up to see a strangely dressed man pouring feed for the horses. He shut his eyes and shook his head as he tried to sit up. "Now, now, easy does it." The man was right next to him. Strong hands steadied him as they sat him up against the wall. Guerdon looked up into the hood that was over his helper's face, but nothing could be seen within. A white hand dipped a cup of water from the water bucket and placed it firmly in Gerdon's hands and lifted it to his lips. "Here, drink." Gerdon was still waking up, thinking that in one final wave of consciousness he would awaken from this dream. The other turned and began walking back toward the feed bucket. He flipped his head covering off and Gerdon saw a head of white hair, and noticed for the first time a hunch in the shoulders that testified of old age. Gerdon thought he must be some old hermit, come down from the mountains. His dress was that of the frosty heights. He wore a floor length parka, made out of a tawny deerskin and fringed in white fur. Gerdon took a good long drink from the cup. He could feel the cool refreshing of the water move into his stomach and then branch out across his entire body. He cleared his throat, "I appreciate your help, but you should know I have nothing to offer you for wages." Still with his back to Japha's father, the old man laughed. "Oh, well, I'm not here for money. I just thought you could use the sleep after everything." He reached his hand up and petted one of Bartain's stable mates. "And these beauties are one of my favorite songs." Guerdon rolled his eyes; he had little love for old men who spoke in riddles. He was feeling very good all of the sudden and stood up. The other, sensing a change in Gerdon's posture, let down his bucket. Gerdon watched in wonder as the person before him turned and faced him. He turned in an odd way, for his back was slightly hunched over and he shuffled as he seemed to pivot on his front end. Gerdon was lost in the soft eyes that gazed upon him. A wrinkled smile was hung quaintly on a loving face. White hair hung around pale skin as it joined a long beard. The one before him reached over and took hold of a staff Gerdon had not noticed before and leaned on it as he let Gerdon inspect him.

Gerdon stood dumb, unable to speak, and completely unaware of a boyish grin that seemed to have crept up on him. White eyelashes framed deep dark eyes, like frost on a window frame when the world is dark outside. Gerdon was drawn to those eyes, which somehow contained the vastness of the stars within them. The features were a bit peculiar, the nose almost catlike. His looks contained an interesting mixture of fierceness and compassion, absolute wisdom and perfect love. Finally, the old man spoke, "Take it easy now, son. I think it was about time you had something to eat." With that he nodded and shuffled about again and started walking toward the house. Gerdon followed and found his limbs strong and ready beneath him. As they entered the house, Gerdon was wafted by the smell of stew simmering over the fire. The old one pulled the pot off the hook and placed it on the table. "I hope you won't mind. I took the liberty of making you an early dinner. The first meal after sorrow can be the hardest." Gerdon sat down at the table, unsure of what was happening, but realizing that he was very hungry, as if he hadn't eaten for a long time. When the steaming bowl was place before him, he looked up in earnest to the one who had served him. "Uh, thank you." He felt awkward saying it, but he couldn't help himself. The ancient eyes closed softly with a flutter of acceptance. He sat down opposite of Gerdon. Gerdon ate slowly, enjoying the stew and resting himself in the moment. It wasn't long before his eyes grew heavy and he began to think of Japha. His precious little girl was lost forever. He let the spoon slip from his hand as he raised it up to cover his eyes.

The other watched silently with understanding and reaching in his pocket pulled out an odd shaped pipe. Gerdon wiped his eyes and looked at the one before him. He suddenly realized that he didn't even know his name or where he was from. He was thankful for his presence now. It was a great comfort to have company. Guerdon greatly feared the cold grasp of loneliness. He mourned the loss of his lovely daughter, yet it was the fear of being alone, totally alone that had truly shattered him. He watched without speaking and with increasing interest as the other filled his pipe with water, not tobacco. He took a great suck on the pipe and then proceeded to blow a steamy cloud ring which hung for just a moment in the air over the table before becoming millions of tiny droplets of water which then fell onto the wooden surface with many little plops. Gerdon stared at the wetness on the table and then back up to the stranger before him. The old one had laughter in his eyes, and spoke with his pipe hanging out of the corner of his mouth. "It's a little too dry in here of you ask me." Gerdon could say nothing, but the display moved him and he began to chuckle despite himself. The one who was with him laughed as well and his laugh was contagious. Gerdon burst out in heaving laughter that lasted for over a minute. When it finally subsided, his ribs hurt and his eyes were brimming with fresh new tears. The old one sat back breathing heavily, "Ahh, yes, that's the way to go now. The only way to usher in a new life is through joy."

Gerdon looked at him now rather seriously. "May I ask who you are?" The dark eyes flashed up at him for an instant with a great sharpness and excitement Gerdon had not expected. It passed quickly enough as the other leaned over the table eyeing the broken man before him. As if he was pondering what the best way would be to answer the question. "I am Three, I am Jedekiah."

Gerdon looked at him intently. He suddenly became aware of many things all at once. The fact that many of the things Jedekiah had spoken to him; had been, it seemed, answers to things he had thought not spoken. The sensation and strength that had come to him from the water he had given him. How familiar his voice was, how it soothed him and awakened something deep within, something that had been buried a long time ago. And many other tiny details of this man flooded his mind and overwhelmed him for a time. At last he was able to speak, "Why are you here?" His voice was barely above a whisper. As if he could not believe the honor, the privilege, the reality of being in the presence of the one who was sitting with him. Jedekiah leaned back and sighed, a deep heavy breath. The atmosphere in the room felt full and rich. He rose from his chair with apparently a bit of effort and motioned to Gerdon to follow him out the door. Night would soon be here and Guerdon saw that they must have been inside for longer than he had realized. Three bright stars could be seen in the horizon. Gerdon gazed up at them. A clap of thunder was heard and Gerdon turned around wondering how long before the storm was upon them. The elder looked at the ground and shuffled his feet, "The storm has been brewing for some time, now. Don't you worry now; you'll not see much damage here." The old one walked with his head down as is he was looking at the ground as he continued, "You've been through a different kind of storm, child." He lifted his head and took in a deep breath. "That's it, when you can smell the rain before you see a cloud, a scent carried in advance by the wind." He turned and looked straight at Gerdon, "My boy, I came here to tell you, that you are going to be alright. The pain of losing your daughter was the final weight that tipped the scales so to speak and brought you to the breaking point. You called out in your despair to me. I have come, and I have helped you wake up." Guerdon wondered what he meant and turned his head as he heard another great clap of thunder.

The ancient one continued to speak, "This storm is from the other shore, and carries within it the beginning of many things. This storm will do it's best to ensure that the old is gone before the new arrives. You will be alone here for a season, but it will not be a long one. You must remember who you are, who you were created to be. Husband, father, friend, horse master: you have born many titles, but they cannot begin to define who you are." The old one took Gerdon's shoulder and looked up into his eyes, "You are my son and I am *with you.*" Gerdon couldn't speak as he was taken into the gaze, drawn deep into his eyes. The vastness of the stars opened up before him and he saw himself there, a tiny part in beautiful expanse of creation. A sweet laugh pulled him back, "Little one, hey, you might be, but you will learn that I am not small and when I am with you, you are not as little as you think."

He walked alongside the other now as they drew near to the first corral. A young horse was trotting around, excited and skittish from the scent of the storm. The old one nodded to the filly. "That one is something special, isn't she?" Guerdon looked at the filly. He had noticed her potential, but had not done much to develop it yet. The Old One nodded in response, "*Yes, a broken man tries in vain. But with new strength, the Way is gained.*" The words came out like the rustle of leaves in the wind. Guerdon was drawn to him and moved up next to Jedekiah as he began walking down a path that led into the trees.

They walked in contented silence, until at last Gerdon's heart again remembered its pain. He turned toward his companion. "Will I ever see my daughter again?" The white lashes fluttered at the question. "My, son, there are some answers that you are simply not ready to hear yet." Guerdon felt a great turmoil within him. Part of him rose up, hopeful murmuring, *yes, yes;* while other parts of him teetered on the edge of despair, *no, never.* He shook his head, he didn't know either way, so there was no use in entertaining either train of thought. The road before them was cool and shaded in the trees. Just ahead a clearing of green grass began to part the forest. Guerdon was looking ahead and did not see the brown bundle he tripped over. He stumbled and grabbed onto Jedekiah's arm. The arm was solid in a way that betrayed the look of age the Old One wore. Guerdon turned his attention to the bag. Picking it up he realized it was Japha's. His eyes were red as he looked down the path, remembering her task to take some of her things to the neighbor's children. He looked to the air and then jogged down to the clearing. The marks of many claws had scratched up the entire field. Guerdon looked around unable to determine the details of Japha's capture. He looked back and saw the robed figure coming up behind him. "Yes, boy. This is where she was taken." Jedekiah now looked around and Guerdon was not prepared for the emotion and heartache he saw on the white face. He was suddenly aware that the one he was with knew and loved his daughter with a depth and power that exceeded what his mortal heart was capable of. The Old One finished his inspection of the scene and turned back toward the path. "Come on, it's time we went back." Guerdon was not sure he was ready to quit the place yet, but began moving in response to the deep voice anyway.

Guerdon slung his daughters bag over his shoulder as they walked. Jedekiah tapped it with his staff. "You'll see that this is the way of many things. One begins a task that another will finish. One man plants a seed that will bear fruit for another to harvest." Guerdon felt the weight of the bag on his shoulder. He would make sure that he honored Japha's intentions for her belongings. Jedekiah began speaking again as if Gerdon's thoughts were a part of a conversation and not a private occurrence. "Yes, intentions are at the heart of everything. Though the action itself may be seen clearly, one's motives are often veiled."

They were soon back at the house and stepped quietly inside. The Old One set his staff aside and sat down, moaning and sighing as if his bones ached. Guerdon eyed him thoughtfully as he let the bag fall off his shoulders. "Why do you do that? If you are who I think you are, you would not ache so." Jedekiah looked up with laughter in his eyes, he enjoyed Gerdon's curiosity. He laughed as he spoke, "Who you think I am, and just what kind of thoughts could those be I wonder." He chuckled as if the very thought of Guerdon contemplating who and what he was, was hilarious. Guerdon was puzzled by this reaction and sat down. He knew he was not meaning to be deceitful, but why give the appearance and attitude of aged flesh when he was strong. "Well, there is a mystery, isn't it. I do not intend to deceive you. I intend to make you comfortable. Indeed it is no lie for me to take on the appearance of aged flesh, for I am ancient. I am not bound by time, though I can move in it, I am ruler over it. But for you to see and accept my presence in your domain I must appear in a manner you will understand. You need my wisdom and understanding of suffering right now, so I come full of years, wearing my experience on my face and body as men do, for your benefit." Guerdon nodded as he took this in. "Try to think of it as what you did with your Japha when she was a child, often you knelt down to speak with her, or lifted her up so you could talk face to face for she was short and you were tall. It is the same, today for you I have knelt down to your level."

Gerdon had many questions, but found that as the evening drew on, the warmth of the room and the presence of his Father were enough to content him and he asked less. He was receiving more from the mere presence of his visitor than from his words. For in Jedekiah he saw the same sweet spirit that brought about the same soothing atmosphere that Japha did. Or was it perhaps, that in Japha he had seen this One? His companion reclined by the fire and gazed at Gerdon, a knowing smile crossed his face, an easy smile that comes when one sees that they have accomplished what was needed to be done.

A dragon sings
With folded wings

They've tried in vain
To bar their pain

The Storm is here
The Dawn so near

Who now can say?
Who knows the Way?

17

Kaxil stormed through the center platform of the Keep, towards his chamber. He was unsettled. He had slapped his dragon affectionately, yet absentmindedly. Farn looked after his rider as he strode away and felt as well as saw a faint glow all around his form. It was new, not like the others, not emanating out of his being, but encasing him so to speak. The dragon had not seen this before but grew content as he felt warmth and joy brush against him as well as he curled up to sleep. Kaxil brushed past Akail who was still asleep along the stone wall. The youth awakened as Kaxil stomped by, unknowingly kicking dust up into Akail's face. He rose silently and went to fetch Kaxil some food and drink.

The sound of other riders voices raised in laughter and jest caused Kaxil to look out of his room. He saw his friends walk by; seemingly unaware of the suffering they were allowing to take place outside of these walls.

Kaxil pulled the curtain shut and threw his riding gloves across his room. He let out a low groan of frustration as he sat and grabbed his head with both hands. Entwining his fingers through his windblown hair, he tried to forget her. His heart was breaking, perhaps for the first time in his life. The face of the little Seafaress, so pure, so lovely, unlike any other he had ever seen. He had seen children before, but never such innocence. And he had taken her to her execution! He could still feel her small body in front of his, shivering in the wind. He wished now that he had offered her some comfort, wrapped his cloak around her or something. He rose and paced around his room. *Why? Why is this affecting me so?* He could find no answer. There was no escaping her eyes; it seemed as if their image had been bored into his very soul. He ripped off his leather-riding vest and splashed his face with cool water. *Get a hold of yourself.* Akail entered, slowly and low to the ground. Nearly on his knees he sought to place the tray on the small table in the corner and leave without disturbing his master. Kaxil noticed him and spoke out to him, eager for some relief from the torments of his conscience. "Akail, please come in." Kaxil had extended his hand out toward the boy and motioned for him to sit on the chair. Akail stood stunned for a moment. Kaxil had never spoken to him in such a way before. He quickly obeyed and eyed his young master carefully, wondering what had caused the change. Kaxil seemed nervous as he sat back down. Now that his slave was sitting attentively, Kaxil wasn't sure exactly what to say to him. The dragon rider brushed his hands down his thighs and then together in front of his face. He finally dropped them and looked at Akail. "I thought we might talk for a moment." Kaxil spoke as if trying to convince himself that this might be an enjoyable way to pass the time. Akail was certain Kaxil must be displeased with him over some small matter. Kaxil was searching his hangings and walls trying to find something to talk about. He finally shut his eyes and put a hand to his forehead. He was shaken, completely shaken. Akail became concerned for his master and dared to ask, "Are you feeling alright, sir?" Kaxil nodded, "Yes, at least I think so…" he began to shake his head, "no, not really, I don't know." His head remained bowed between his hands. The page reached for the cup of wine he had brought on the tray and stepped silently over to the troubled man. Kaxil felt a soft touch on his should and raised his head to see Akail standing near him. "Here sir." Kaxil accepted the wine and watched Akail thoughtfully as the youth turned and moved back to his seat. It suddenly occurred to him that Akail held, in another manner, an air and sweetness that he had seen in the girl. He now realized he did not even know from what country his charge was from. "Who are your people Akail?" The boy shifted uneasily in his chair. He did not want it to be commonly known that he was from the Shore country. It might contribute to undesired beatings from the other pages and riders. Sea Folk were often seen as the lowest sect among men. Kaxil simply nodded when the boy failed to reply. "I thought so." Akail's eyes began to water; no doubt nothing good could come from his master's sudden interest in him.

The rider was becoming curious now about this boy's story and life and people. Kaxil sighed heavily and looked at the ground as he spoke, "Akail, do you know what I did today?" Akail looked squarely at his master as he answered, "Yes." Kaxil shifted around again. "I'm glad you are from the Shore country, I'm glad, Akail." Akail was puzzled by Kaxil's behavior. Kaxil continued to speak, "I'm glad I will not be the only one around here who is grieved by what we have done." Akail was unsure of what to say or do for the Sackeen dragon rider who sat before him, full of remorse.

Within the darkness of the Keep, a two glowing beams moved freely and unnoticed, shrouded from those who might *see* them.

The Light found its destination within Kaxil's room. The two guardians who had watched over the dragon rider for so many years received instructions. This was a special moment. Winel pulled a small vial from his belt and poured out a single golden drop of oil onto Kaxil's head. He and his second then spread their wings and cast a shadow of light over the man whose heart was being broken. Laying great hands on his shoulders they called to Kaxil's spirit, and awakened it. A strange peace then fell in the room and Akail and Kaxil began to speak freely as brothers. Across the Keep in his den, Farn began to hum a soft tune in his sleep.

Aylia sat against a wall gazing up at the small window nearly twenty feet above them. They had been herded into one large cell. Oya lay on the stone floor next to her. Aylia reached over and let her hand run through Oya's hair. Her large beautiful eyes gazed up at the tiny dust particles that danced in the rays of sunshine. How she wanted to be part of that dance rather than the one she was a part of. She retreated into herself. Deep within her heart, she listened and found within her a well. She tapped into the reservoir that had been built within her and she heard a Song of the sea. It moved through her, up her throat and out her mouth. Warmth filled the room, rising up and out the window, seeking the source of the sunlight.

> You made the land, before time began.
> You made the Sea, and those who dwell in thee.
> Come shine on me, oh light of distant shores
> Come shine on me, so I will cry no more.
> You made the moon, to give us light at night
> And you'll turn the tide, to take yourself a bride.
> Come shine on us, o light of distant shores
> Come shine on us, that we may soon be yours.

The room was filled with peace and the light from the window seemed to bend down and touch the tired faces of each one of them. Oya had sat up as Aylia had sung. Oya touched her new found friends hand, "Aylia, you have the gift of song!" Aylia seemed to awaken out of a dreamy state and noticed all eyes were on her: sleepy, happy, tired eyes that looked thankfully to her. The place trembled and great shrieks and screams were heard. Unmentionable calls of strange eerie voices filled the caverns and the girls all huddled together in wonder of what was happening. Aylia surprised everyone when she giggled. "I don't think they like my song." The rest responded with a ripple of laughter, the kind that bubbles out uncontrollable. They continued to speak and laugh and cry as they all began to tell of their family and home. One by one they drifted off to sleep as the heat of the day came. Aylia was the last to drift off and as she did, like a warm shower of softly cascading snow, she thought she saw many tiny feathers falling in the cavern.

Many tales are spun and told
About the youth of things now old
Beginnings lost, the end now near
The battle cries of things we fear
Fill our heart and steal our hope
The darkness grows,
How do we cope?
Look for the dawn,
Seek out the Light!
No might can now undo a Sight.
What you held, you now release
To fight the war, take hold of Peace.

18

Kaxil stood alone on a stone balcony. He gazed out over the sea as the sun began to sink behind the Veil in front of him. He felt awake, as if he had been reborn. Everything felt different, yet he knew the change was in him not the world around. He felt life, true life flowing through him, and he gazed at the Light behind the Veil and he felt for the first time as if he knew where home was.

Lost in his own thoughts he did not perceive the soft footfalls behind him. "There is something about it, isn't there, so mysterious what *they* call the Veil." Kaxil turned and was surprised to see the hooded figure beside him. The red hood covered the slight figure of the Searcher who had been assigned to the Keep to show the dragons their charges. Kaxil had never had any liking for the mysterious arts of the Searchers, especially when they messed with his dragon. Yet the present situation was even more of a strain on Kaxil. Searchers were not numerous and held in high esteem, yet they were little more than interpreters and seers. They spoke with the trolls, and fairies, dragons and other creatures which could see into the dim realms as they could more than they spoke with people. "How mundane your life must be when the Kingdom is at peace, herding little Sea Folk around to keep them in line." The woman sighed and rubbed her hands together as if she could feel the dirt of a race that would not convert upon her hands. Kaxil chose not to reply, her words caused him pain and he knew she could not understand why. Kaxil shifted uncomfortably in her presence and looked back into the shadows of the Keep behind him. Across the valley of stone he saw Akail carrying on with his tasks. The Searchers sharp eyes followed Kaxil's then suddenly darted back to the rider beside her as he turned back to the sea. He did not see her face or the way she eyed him with a bit of morbid curiosity before she turned her full attention now to the Keep behind her. A few riders and servants were milling around, dinners were being served and a dragon could be heard bellowing here and there. Yet, something had caught her attention and she was caught by the presence of a bright light, small but alive, moving below. Her *Eye* crept out from the folds of her hood and wrapped itself around her head. It's large orb of and eye stationed itself over her forehead and opened with a fiery orange glow. Smoke like tendrils overshadowed her face, contorting her features with a dark vapor. She let out a cry, a shriek and Kaxil turned at the sound. She whirled around to leave the balcony, her face a sinister version of its former self, and upon turning she came face to face with Kaxil and flinched and cried out again, this time in pain as her *Eye* unmasked the rider, as a shining one, before her unsuspecting gaze. Regaining her wits she lunged with claw like fingers at the glimmering man and his guardians that were before her. A soldier's reflexes caught her as Kaxil protected himself in confusion of the change that now possessed her. And a voice filled his head, strong, steady, authoritative and confident, "Knock her out, but do not kill her." Kaxil, much to his own surprise, obeyed and the Searcher fell into a heap of red fabric on the ground.

Kaxil stared, not knowing what had happened or why. Then he saw a pair of feet, standing beside the sleeping Searcher. They seemed to be made of gold and were in the shape of eagles claws. Kaxil looked up and saw standing before him a

Lightbearer with sword drawn gazing at him in earnest. "Kaxil, you and the boy are no longer safe here. Take him and flee. We will lead you to safety." The words were spoken by the same voice that he had heard a moment before and he nodded and ran down the stairs behind the ethereal being before he had a chance to think it over.

Kaxil hit the bottom of the stairs with such speed that he skidded and nearly lost his balance. He caught himself quickly and proceeded with a bit more caution to his room. He rang the bell for Akail to tend to him and began shoving things into a small pack. While donning his riding jacket and sword he did this he reached out to Farn. *Farn, get up. We're leaving, keep* **quiet,** *to everyone!* Farn answered, *I'm awake and so is the woman.* Kaxil pulled back his curtain door and gazed upon the sight of another rider upon the balcony helping the Searcher to her feet. Kaxil scanned the basin like hall in front of him. Where was Akail?

The Searcher, Nafari, was shouting orders, despite the throbbing of her head where the strange rider had struck her. Her *Eye* lay dead from the blow. She was filled with a vengeful rage. How could she have missed it, in the Dragon's Keep, one who should have been marked months ago! If she moved quickly perhaps they could get the young Sea man to the Capital city in time for the ceremony. Perhaps then, she would not suffer to great reprimand for her *blindness.* The rider, she thought, would be another matter. Never had there been such a threat, a dragon rider, *illuminated* by the other shore? She shoved the implications and enigma surrounding the rider out of her thoughts for now and turned back to searching for the young man.

Kaxil watched the Searcher move through the Bowl sending riders and slaves in every direction as she went. He looked back, the passage to the balcony was nearly empty, everyone seemed to be moving in the other direction.

"Order all dragons grounded! No one is to leave this place!" Nafari barked to the highest ranking rider she could get her hands on.

Akail watched from behind a jutting of stone as a group ran by. He turned and tried to stay in the shadows as he made his way back to Kaxil's apartment. He felt an overwhelming impulse to remain unseen, though he could give no reason for his actions as he moved through the dark slave halls. At a bend in one such passage he was pulled off his feet before he ever reached his destination.

Nafari was holding a damp rag to the small cut that was continuing to drop blood down her brow despite her protests. She was being questioned quite briskly about sending the Keep into such an uproar. "You've got everyone running around searching, for they don't even know who! Now I demand to know what's going on!" The seasoned rider stood steaming waiting for her reply. Nafari stood composed, who was this rider to speak to her, a Priestess of the Eye, in such a way. Her answer began calmly enough but soon her anger rose and overtook her, "I saw a servant, working here in the Keep, a child of the Sea Folk, of the kind that is to be sacrificed in the temple at Ohim. But before I could encounter him one of your riders, whom has fallen into corruption, attacked me! Now I want that boy and the head of your rider. *Now*!!!" Her voice resonated with a hollow depth that shook the core of those in the room.

Akail ran up the stairs behind Kaxil, up to the very balcony the rider had fled from only moments before. At the top Kaxil stopped and peeked around the stone pillar. There was a guard left there. A moment later, Akail watched in awe as his master pulled the unconscious guard out of their way. Akail followed Kaxil to the balcony. Kaxil motioned for him to stay down and Akail crouched below the stone railing. Kaxil kneeled beside him and kept one eye on the stairway, "We have to leave now Akail, I think she *Saw* you somehow." Kaxil's eyes fell for a moment in wonder as he realized that she had *Seen* him too. He didn't have time to look for understanding at the moment. *Farn! Where are you?* Kaxil called out to his dragon. *I'm nearly to you. I follow the shining one.* Kaxil turned to Akail, "I hope you're not afraid of the water." Kaxil motioned over the ledge, "because we're swimming out of here." Akail watched as Kaxil secured his gear. Akail sat in a dumbfounded shock. Kaxil was freeing him, and more than that, he was leaving the Keep with him. Akail shook his head, "We'll never make it." Kaxil was smiling, "Yes we will, he said all we have to do is follow the light." The boy wondered at the attitude of the man before him. Kaxil said, "Now is the time for action, Akail, explanations will have to come later." Akail suddenly realized his freedom was before him, and nodded. Kaxil grabbed Akail's arm and swung him over the balcony onto a small stone ledge and then followed himself.

The wind blasted and the steep stone face descended below them many feet until it ran into the Sea. Light from the sunset behind the Veil poured over them in a soft orange hue. Farn could now be seen crawling up the mountain rock face toward them. It took a bit of maneuvering for them to get onto the long neck but they did and held on as Farn jumped into the air and spread his great wings for only a moment then tucked them and dove for the water just beyond the crashing waves.

The Keep continued to bustle with the activity of the search into the night. Eventually the dragons were sought and it was discovered that Farn and Kaxil were missing. Yet, when asked to call to him, the dragons could get no answer from him. Riders were finally dispatched, but the Sea concealed them well from the sight and scent of other dragons. Farn faithfully carried his cargo like a living ship through the waves as he followed the glowing orbs that drifted purposefully in front of him.

Sandaled feet stepped down the stone stairs. Around empty corners, to find empty posts, and so continued. Sagis walked with an air of nobility, but much of his time was spent in these dark caverns, which had caused him to form strange personal habits that contradicted his air. He often walked on his tiptoes, and carried his lavish robes high above his ankles. He moved past quiet chambers and stopped as he wondered at the silence. He walked on alone. He wanted one last look at the strange children of the Shore who had caught the watchful gaze of the Searchers.

Sagis was intrigued to see that most of the youths were asleep. Two appeared to be speaking and smiling at each other. He found this most unusual. He stopped and listened but could not make out what they were saying. One of the girls turned and saw him. Japha watched as the man approached. He was unlike any other man she had ever seen. He was old and hard. There was no love in him, only power, a hollow power. His ears were full of odd rings. On his bare scalp he had many strange markings. He seemed more like an empty skin walking around, only a thin outline of a man, devoid of the fullness of soul and spirit that made a person at all pleasing to look at. Japha felt sickened as he approached and hoped she would not vomit. She felt she knew things she could not remember being taught. The man now stood tall on the opposite side of the bars. The image struck Japha; it appeared as if he was in a prison. She was filled with a wave of courage and she watched and waited for him to speak first. Aylia looked at the man and realizing the end was near trembled as a tear crept out of her eye. Aylia watched as the man contemplated the foreigners before him. Japha was wondering if he would speak at all. A question swelled up within her and spilled out over her lips. "Do you wish to be free?" The man opened his eyes wide and looked at her. He practically spat his reply, "Freedom cannot be granted by one who is bound." He had not expected such wit from the child. Words poured out of Japha like a tumbling brook. Aylia thought her voice sounded like the ripples and she watched and listened. "These chains and bars have no power over spirit, that which is born of the spirit is spirit and cannot be bound by iron. And so I ask you, do you wish to be free?" Sagis did not fully grasp the meaning of the words, but it seemed the girl did possess some understanding of the spiritual realms. He replied, "I serve my master." Japha felt a great sadness wash over her. She closed her eyes and then looked back to him, "Would you be free from the master that binds you?" Sagis could not understand. His submission to his dark lords had gained him success and power. He looked at the bars in front of him and the huddled captives that lay in balls on the floor. "Is this the measure of your master's power?" Japha looked at the man. A deep stirring was occurring within her.

Light swirled within the pool of her heart. Words of wisdom were being washed up on the shore of her mind. Japha spoke again, "The scales of this land, cannot measure what comes from the other shore." Sagis felt a deep boom, a penetration, an assault against those within him and he shook uncontrollably. He heard within his head many angered voices, *"Do not listen, she lies, she lies."* Others were screaming, *"Kill her, kill her."* Sagis leaned forward and took hold of the bars. *"She lies, a liar, stupid liar."* Japha stepped back at the bidding in her heart. She wished she could get far away from this place. She was upon a battlefield she had not chosen for herself and wavered for just a moment, as she doubted everything she had said. Sagis lifted his head and smiled at her. His face was different and his eyes had lost their whites. He extended his hand out toward her and let out an unintelligible call. All the youth shook and awoke from their sleep. They shuffled around to get away from the mad man. Sagis was laughing, laughing uncontrollably. "You are all doomed!"

Loved ones are taken
Such is the cost

The prize that is won
The souls of the lost

19

Aylia was first in line out into the courtyard which was vast and full of a great crowd of people. Many were dressed well for the day's festivities. Aylia and the others had never seen so many Sackeen civilians. In her village she had only ever seen soldiers. Her eyes passed over the crowd and she wondered if things may be different if even one of them, just one of them might have thought of her as friend. Their voices sounded like the rushing waves of the sea. And she closed her eyes for she could hear no words. The sound of the water, their voices were all around her, there was no truth, no hope hidden within the sound. She saw the man Sagis standing at the back of the platform as they were lined up, beside a large stone table. Sagis stepped in front of it and put his arms up. A strange silence flooded over the crowd. Aylia looked back over the line of her sisters and brothers. They were all afraid, despite the hope they had found in each other. Sagis took hold of a large pitcher and a cup and poured a dark substance. He held the cup over his head and began to call upon his gods. The crowd began to chant and cheer. Another, like Sagis, yet less important came and touched their foreheads with fingers he dipped in a red substance. Drums pounded.

There was a shriek and crack as something began to break through the stone ground of the courtyard. The crowd moved to the walls and a great design upon the floor could be seen, it appeared like the markings of an ancient gate.

In the back of the courtyard was a large group of people. They moved to the place where the governors and officials were sitting. A stir began in the people and shouts of rage mingled with the threats of posted guards filled the air. Tension grabbed hold and electricity filled the air. Even Sagis stopped his prayers to look over to see what was causing the interruption. The shaven head of a temple dweller was seen bobbing by the guards, up the stairs and onto the raised ramp that encircled the courtyard. He scurried more than ran, but quickly reached the main platform. He approached Sagis and spoke into his ear. Aylia tried to hear what he said but the roar of the crowd was too much. Sagis placed the cup down and turned and looked with great indignation toward the rulers. He took a few paces across the platform and then shouted, "If there is such a One, let him come forward!"

Aylia's mouth felt dry. She could not see what was happening within the group at the other end of the courtyard. There seemed to be much movement and shuffling around. She closed her eyes tight and took in a deep breath. The expanse above held a bright blue sky; there was not a cloud to be seen. Curiosity had now eclipsed her sorrow and dread for a moment. No tears formed in her eyes. There was no water, no words, only the unending murmur of a multitude of people that were as unaware of what was occurring as she was.

Moving across the stone door which was the floor, there at last appeared a man in red. He was moving slowly with an entanglement of Sackeen guards behind him. When they approached the bottom of the stairs Sagis threw his hand out in front of him. The man stopped and stood. Aylia looked with wide eyes down the long steps. The man was not wearing red, but was drenched in it. He stood unbound with his hands slightly raised from his sides, and his head bowed down. Sagis stepped tenderly down half of the stairs and peered at this blood soaked intruder. Sagis spoke quietly at first, "You have so come of your own will?" The man looked up at him. "I have." Aylia gasped as she recognized the man, it was Barduuk! Sagis stepped closer and touched the hem of Barduuk's tunic and smelt his fingers. Blood. Barduuk's face was badly beaten. Sagis could only guess at the wounds, concealed by the shirt, and yet obvious by the amount of blood absorbed by it. "Who did this to you?" Sagis wanted names, wanted to know who had forced this man here. Barduuk answered vaguely, "I have endured much to achieve… my destination." Sagis squinted at him. He was not mad, his speech was clear. He was tired and beaten, but still well alive. Sagis looked out at the crowd, rubbing his fingers together in the blood of the stranger before him. Calculating his next move, he watched the crowd, and pondered the laws and customs of the people. Barduuk spoke again, with a clear and loud voice, "I have claimed my destiny. Will you deny me it?" Sagis glanced at the man again and then back to the crowd. He turned without a word and strode up the stairs. His subordinate stood by the table. Sagis drew near. Keeping his back to the crowd he bent his head down and the other spoke into his ear once again. Sagis lifted his head and spoke something quickly to the other, then spun around. He looked with great pleasure now on the man at the bottom of the steps. His eyes filled with dark desire. Now here before him was the one he had sought to undo. He motioned for preparations to be made. He then raised his hands and called for the attention of the crowd. "My fellow Sackeens, a Cupbearer has come forth! According to our ancient laws, this man offers himself in the office of a cupbearer to any who will accept him." A tumult of cries and cheers, some angry others astonished rose and filled the open sanctuary.

Sagis let the crowd have its roar and then lifted his hands for silence yet again. What did this mean? Who was this man? No one had seen a Cupbearer, not for over a hundred years! How did this man come to know of the forgotten right? Questions and assumptions were spreading already. Sagis grabbed his staff and pounded it upon the stone. When it hit the ground the top of the staff opened up and black bladelike projections came out and formed the insignia of the gods. A hush fell. Sagis looked down at the man before him. He motioned and the blood stained man proceed up the steps. He then turned toward the group of Sea Folk youth behind him. His dark eyes were filled with curiosity and revelry. He spoke darkly, "Do any of you accept this man?" his gaze fell first to Aylia who stood closest to him. She returned his gaze with a questioning look. Time seemed to slow down to a crawl. Aylia looked at Barduuk, and saw everything that he was at once, and she knew she could not deny him, even this. All that he was, and would be, and had been she accepted and believed in, so without fully understanding what would happen she answered, "Yes." Sagi turned, he was satisfied. He needed only one to agree. Aylia began to feel an odd sensation all over her body knew rain had begun to fall softly. Yet she stood there, unmoving, among the others and watched as Barduuk took her cup.

A cry, a call
In death to fall

The end we fear
Is now so near

The past is gone
The future is won

20

Barduuk was chained down on the table. Sagis took the cup again, and again began the ceremony. Aylia's mouth quivered as she watched and understood what was happening. *Not like this!* He had told her she would see him again. *On the other shore, I thought. In the Light, in another place.*

As the cup was brought to Barduuk's lips, he looked into the liquid as he had done on the Other Shore in a before time. He sat at the edge of water with his Father. He had looked at the still sea. The voice of his Father caused the liquid to tremble before him. "What do you see?" His Father pointed to their reflections upon the water. Light was all around him and he answered, "I see a great lion, with a mane of gold that burns like fire. The head shines like the sun and the moon hangs from his tail. When he walks thunder rumbles and when he roars lightening comes from his mouth." His Father had smiled and taken a cup and handed it to his son. Barduuk had looked into it. A liquid that appeared like blood and smelt of suffering threatened to spill over the edge. The Father had spoken again, "What do you see here?" Gazing into the cup he had seen the face of a lamb, broken and bleeding, dying, reflecting up toward in upon the red liquid. He told his Father what he had seen with a troubled look on his face. He had gazed back into the cup as the vision changed, "Now I see faces, beyond number, faces full of joy, love, some twisted in pain and anguish. I hear them calling out to you, I hear them calling a name, my name." As he had gazed into the cup his heart had been undone. In that instant love burst and blossomed, a consuming passionate love for every face. In that moment he also felt the pain of losing them. Sorrow and mourning engulfed him, causing the first tear to fall upon that distant shore. The drop made ripples in the water and the first waves were born.

Again tears rolled down Barduuk's face, this time leaving dirty streaks down his face. He drank deeply of the cup.

Aylia stood numbly looking at the motionless body of the man who had bought her life. Aylia lifted her eyes to Sagis. The man stood backed up against the doorway behind him. He looked mad, dazed and confused. His eyes rested on Barduuk's body, his conquest. He had achieved the death of the Sea Folk miracle worker. He began to shiver and sway, reaching his hands out to the tiny doorframe for support.

The drums continued, louder and felt deeper. The ground shook. Sagis stepped forward and began to chant and call in an unknown language. The rain fell like a light mist and a loud rumble of thunder boomed through the atmosphere. The door that was lying down upon the earth split from the sides of the stones and a dark crack appeared. Out from the blackness, steam escaped as if the earth released a long held breath. Screams and howls were then heard and a call rang out that caused the crack to split. Great black claws were then seen, reaching out and apparently trying to tear open the earth from within. Many terrible voices escaped the crack revealing a multitude that dwelt deep in the darkness. People were screaming with shrieks of terror, but they could not escape the nightmare they had come to see. Soon the claws prevailed against the stone floor and underlying dirt. They were followed by a large beak and a head of white feathers.

Aylia's eyes were held open by the sight in front of her. She had never witnessed such a spectacle. Calling the hidden things was forbidden among the Sea Folk. The large head of an owl emerged from the hole, and beneath it came two powerful, manlike, shoulders. But here the beast struggled again, caught apparently in the opening that would be his escape. It squirmed and clawed at the ground, now using its beak to break apart the stones around it. And Aylia began to notice that it seemed to be working toward a goal, in the direction of the stone table, upon which Barduuk's body lay. It stretched toward the red man upon the table and gave a challenging call. Aylia gasped in horror as Sagis stepped forward and welcomed the beast and invited it to come partake of the feast he had laid before it on this table. Aylia cried out, "NOOO!" as she realized that Barduuk's body was to be consumed by the creature. Sagis glanced at her and smiled. There was nothing to be done now. His friend would have his prize.

The ground shook as the beasty writhed to break free of the doorway. The tumult of its struggling cries was broken as the sky parted in the east. It seemed as if the very sunset was reversed and the light was traveling back across the sky toward the land. The light broke into pieces and the foremost two of these luminaries began to spin and grow as they drew near. They were beautiful to behold, similar and yet separate. All eyes were taken away as these uninvited quests descended onto the temple area. The forms of two women, clothed in white feathers, each wielding a feathered staff, maneuvered within the lights. The second light landed above Sagis, on the peak of the roof. The first light alighted directly in front of the stone table. She landed in a crouching position, yet gathered herself up to a standing position with her eyes fixed upon the under-worldly intruder. Only Japha and Aylia had ever seen the likes of her before. Wisdom established herself, in all her glory, between the monster from the depths and the body of Barduuk. She cocked her head just enough to let her opponent know that he was her target.

The ground shook again, as the owl like being began to tremble and growl in rage. Wisdom and Understanding leapt into the air in one fluid movement. Understanding moved behind Wisdom, in synchronized motion. One great summer-salt and a swift sweep of their staff's and Wisdom landed as before, yet she was in the center of the arena now, and the head of the great fowl from beneath rolled on the stone floor. Understanding had lighted in front of the table where Wisdom had been. The first stood again and turning set her face toward those on the stairs. Aylia met her gaze and the image of light and beauty was forever burned into her spirit. Into the black pools that lied in the center of Wisdoms eyes, Aylia perceived the depths of the ages. Later she would try to explain what she saw as a starry night that seemed never to end and yet moved like the sea, as if it was alive and breathed.

Rain descended in large drops and as the water touched the crowned beauties their light diminished and was then unseen. A loud clap of thunder seemed to split the clouds and release the seas of the sky. There now was no trace of Wisdom's victim, safe a few large feathers.

There seemed to be much going on, as people ran and scurried here and there. The leaders were nowhere to be seen. Sagis stood on the precipice gazing at the small crack that remained. He had seen his god, and had seen it beheaded. He gazed at Barduuk's body, he had his victory. Then what had happened, why the beast not prevailed in achieving his prize: feasting on the flesh of his sacrifice. He had performed this ceremony before, and never had anything challenged the powers of this world in such a way. Sagis' dark eyes spanned across the city toward the sea in unanswerable wonder, and the coldness of the falling water kept his senses stark awake in this scenario that he wished to awaken from as if a dream.

Water falls, for water calls

Come and cleanse, carry deep
All his tears to those who sleep

The Dawn will go invade the Night
What is wrong will be made right.

21

Akail stood with his hand on Farn's back. The dragon was singing. Akail smiled as he listened. Whatever had caused such a great change in Kaxil was affecting his dragon as well. They had taken to the air at dawn the preceding morning and traveled far across the country. They were camped in the wilderness and the three fugitives were about to eat when the storm hit. They were able to find shelter in a dense patch of forest nearby, but the storm lasted all night and no fire was able to be kindled, even by dragon breath, for the ferocity of the wind and rain.

Water fell without regard for the splat it became on the stone streets of the Capital city. The rain was washing Barduuk's blood soaked garments. A red river poured down the steps and was carried down into the earth by the drains. Aylia stood dazed. It was Oya who got them moving, amidst the crowd when everyone else was looking elsewhere. She led them out of the courtyard and herded them into an abandoned booth just outside the wall. The group had managed to escape virtually unnoticed. Oya gazed out into the rain that formed a gray veil that now covered everything in sight. The streets soon emptied of people as the rain came down in a threatening force. Aylia listened to it. It sounded angry, very angry and her small body shivered in fear.

After a short while, something was heard out in the rain. A splat, tap on the street. A few of the girls sat up and leaned forward. The shape of a person could now be seen huddled beneath a coat. It seemed as if he emerged from the rain itself. Fahim stood with his hands held high, holding his coat over his head. He stared with wide eyes at the group of forgotten girls. His mouth formed a crooked smile, as if only half of it was able to, the other half was drooped in disbelief. *There they are!* He took a deep breath and looked around. Nothing could be seen through the gray drizzle that was cascading all around them. He turned back to the group of young Sea Folk. Leaning forward he spoke loudly, "Come with me, I have a place you can stay." The girls shifted uneasily. Some were shocked, others surprised, yet all of them were daring to believe that they were now on the other side of doom. Hope was battering at the doors of their hearts that had now gone into mourning and shock. Oya looked at the others, she was most likely the oldest. Stepping up she thought the others would follow. They did. The man introduced himself quickly, "My name is Fahim! Follow me." He assured them that his place was not far. Aylia remembered turning once or twice in the journey. They saw no one.

The storm raged on as the refugees tramped down the street toward a safe haven. The man led them to a small lodge. A warm fire was waiting and all twelve youths piled into a small lounge area. The wood floor was soon soaked as they dripped. Fahim hung his coat up and turned around. He was tall and thin, probably in his thirties. He tried to flash his shivering guests a smile but turned and called, "Jiaya! I found them!" They were given dry clothes and a room was prepared for them. They were all too much in shock to remember much, but later Aylia would be able to recall a part of the conversation from the dinner table. Fahim had spoken, "The tide has turned." Oya seemed to talk a great deal with him about many things, yet it was his manner of speaking that Aylia noticed. He spoke with confidence about what had happened that day, not sorrow. "They are strange and wonderful days indeed that we are living in, when our dreams flood the reality of our waking."

Later that night, dry and safe, Aylia rested her head on a soft pillow. Her eyes could cry no more tears and she realized that sky as well, had given all its water. The rain stopped pounding in the roof, but in the distance Aylia could still hear the rumbling of distant thunder. A deep sleep came over her and if she dreamed she did not remember it.

The sound of voices, loud and excited, filled with awe awoke Aylia. She could see through the window that the sun was breaking through the clouds that had lingered from the storm. As Aylia made her way down the stairs she was surprised to see Fahim bidding a handful of people farewell at the door. He turned around and strode quietly to the head of the table. Fahim gripped the back of his chair until his knuckles turned white. He then looked around. "I believe that we should grab a bite to eat and head to beach." No one questioned him, and soon they were joining a large crowd that bobbed down the street like a river.

Aylia had not felt like walking that morning. Tired and broken she had trudged on in silence amidst the others.

When they reached the crowded shore, Aylia exclaimed in surprise. The Sea of her dreams lay exposed before her. The sun shone upon the open waters of a vast ocean. Hundreds stood in wonder as they gazed out at the waves. The Veil that had for centuries hidden the horizon from view, was now gone. In the light of the dawn, nothing could be seen but the apparently endless blue of the water. The new phenomenon drew many to the shore that day and for many weeks and months afterward. For more astonishing than the loss of the Veil, were the strange lights that glittered in the night sky. A strange shimmer of brilliance, that testified of a source of light that resided on the other side of the Sea.

Strength that is strong
Right turned to wrong

A heart that will glow
So that you will know

22

Koim was moving through a thick crowd. The Tower city was bustling. It was only the second day after the great storm that had battered the entire Shore. Docks were lost, boats destroyed, homes, crops had been ravaged. The sound of many people making repairs and searching for help filled the morning. The sun was bright and he squinted as he looked around. He was unsure of his surroundings. It didn't take him long to locate the entrance to the Tower. The large stonewalls remained unmoved by the waves and wind of the tempest. Koim waited for hours as crowds swamped the area seeking help from the Temple Priests. Koim stood still within the crowd that moved and bobbed like the sea and looked up at the immense tower that apparently rose to meet the heavens above.

Hiss and moan
Screech and howl

Shadows dark
Enjoy this hour

When Light has come
'Be bound remain'

A victory chorus
Who could refrain?

Yet, what is this?
No chains can hold

And the Keys release
Captives of old.

23

Although the water from the heavy rains was no longer visible, it was not gone. It had simply descended, trickling, winding, and falling again and again down into the deep caverns of the earth. Carrying with it the blood from stone table, from the body of the one who had drank from the cup. That blood, the blood of the innocent man, cried out for his soul, and the soul followed. It traveled beyond sight and time into darkness. Down, to the very gates of Hell. And standing on that precipice of stone he faced the Liar and Father of lies. The Spirit of Barduuk remained and waited on the edge of a great canyon within the depths. On the far side powerful fingers gently caressed a set of intricate keys that hung from a scepter. Cries of anguish were mingled and nearly drowned out by calls and howls of victory. The greatest Bearer of Forgotten Light on the shore of men was now to be locked forever in the prison of Justice. The Keys would see to that. The one who held the Keys to death and Hades had the authority and right to release death and exact punishment for life. The only power greater was the Word of the one who had made the Keys.

The dark seraph strode confidently over to a large mechanism that was used in the forging of chains. He smiled; his eternal guest would become his favorite centerpiece. These chains were not made by men or by the understanding of men. They were forged with the blood of the deceased, which bore the testimony of their life and deeds and so bound them. That blood which had given them life above, now bound them below. Strange hands moved, silhouetted by the celestial flames, taking bowls that rested beneath cracks in the stone, collecting the water and blood that had traveled so far. The red liquid glistened in the firelight as it was poured into a tiny canal, which led to the smoldering pot. Shackles were forged, of a strange design, circles within circles: moving parts that began to whirl, as if *grasping* for their purpose. Carried across the canyon they were placed around the base of the soul. The Lie stood victorious in the darkness and his laugh filled the chasm, resonating throughout the canyon below and the caves above.

The vapor-like Barduuk spoke not a word but simply raised his hand. A simply bidding gesture and a single light shone in the darkness, as the first star appears in the sky at even. The chains unwound and opened from his feet and rose until his hand grasped them. The material in his hand burst in a golden light as it was remade. The sight of the light caused the laughter to cease and the one who laughed to pause and look in wonder. The chains had not been broken; they had opened, without the Keys? How could this be? Barduuk answered, as he watched a bow form in his hands unwinding from the shackles like a scroll, the sound of his voice made waves that shook the earth he stood within. "You should have pondered my blood more closely." His enemy turned toward the bowl that had held the blood. He strode over in anxious fright and looked within. What was happening? The bowl was empty save for a thin layer that still clung to the sides. A black claw like finger touched it. He pulled back as searing pain flooded from his finger through his being like a surge of electricity. His finger smoldered and burned like the flesh of men when touched by hot coals. He did not understand it. He had never seen blood that had such properties before. It even smelt strange. The heat of the earth was causing the water to evaporate, and the blood rose with it in the steam. Not bound by the weight of dark deeds, the remnant of blood in the bowl rose! This had never been seen before.

The source of the clean blood spoke again, and again the earth shook. Great balls of rocks cascaded and cries of distress rose within the deep. "I am *Innocent*." Realization came to eyes of fire and the serpent of flame ignited in wrath. Barduuk as well became engulfed in light as he leapt into the air. The flaming snake met him over the great canyon and hues of blue, gold, and white collided with gold and red. The bow in the man's hand flared in white light and blazed into a sword of living rays. The explosion of light was followed by a tumult of hues as light overcame darkness. Down into the secret places of the world they struggled. The light of the sword filled the depths and the earth began to moan like a woman giving birth.

Ophinum lay on his back, closing his eyes to the light of his doom. "Open your eyes and behold the First Born!" Ophinum opened his eyes and saw what was possible. For a soul to be justly free from his grasp. Free to return, free to live on, no longer subject to Death, but a lord over it. How could this be, he had supplanted the First Born centuries ago! How could a dead man become a First? The First among mankind spoke again, "I am not alone; you will see my blood again and again for I am to offer it and its healing properties to any and all who will receive it. Beware of my brothers and sisters, for if you come against me, you will stir up the full extent of my love which will awaken my wrath." His foe wriggled and moaned within his grasp. Smoke and vapor rose from him as if he was being deflated. His eyes bulged as he beheld him. *A man, he is a man, a human. How can this be? Mankind was mortal!* Barduuk pulled his face down next to those flickering eyes of flame, "I am a man, but know this, Mankind can now be released into their destiny.

Your power over them will be broken by my blood and in my name! I am the First of Many." With that he called to the Keys and they responded. Abandoning one who had held them for so long, they took their rightful place in the hand of the Barduuk and he became the Last the Hold the Keys, for his grip, now, could never be broken. And so it was there in the darkness and the depths that the dark seraph was the first to see Barduuk as the First and the Last.

The first rays of a new dawn for man shone within the depths of Hell before they burst upon the face of the earth. One by one cells were opened and chains unlocked within the Third Prison. Barduuk fulfilled a promise that was made before time began, and so he released from the darkness those who had preceded him on this mortal Shore. And Hell was shaken as it gave up its greatest price, the souls of the righteous.

Taken away,
    No reason to stay.

    My hope has now gone
        To mourn is not wrong

        But I have been shown
I am not alone.

24

Kaxil woke to the quiet clear morning that was peeking through the dark shroud of the forest. He stood and stretched. The phrase, "Take him home." Kept running through his head and he had the faintest remembrance of a dream. Kaxil looked around, Farn lay, awake but unmoving while Akail was starting a small fire. "Akail," Kaxil walked over slowly, "do you know where your home is?" Akail stopped in his work and looked up. His eyes fell, "No, I was small and I can't remember. I see images in my memories, if I saw it I would know it, but I do not know my way home." He spoke with futility as someone who had tried but could not succeed.

Kaxil squatted and stared at the fire for a few minutes. His thoughts drifted to his dragon, *Farn? How did we find the home of the girl? How did you know where to go?* Farn snorted, the thought of trying to explain the thoughts and sights of dragons to men was often difficult and so dragons rarely attempted it. Yet he answered Kaxil as best he could, *I was shown.* Kaxil thought about this while he chewed on the end of a small stick. *The Searcher showed you?* Farn answered again, *Yes.* Kaxil kept thinking. The woman had seen, had seen the girl, as she must have seen Akail before she turned on Kaxil on the balcony. And having seen her home she somehow showed the images to the dragons and they were able to find the locations. Kaxil wondered, *Farn, how much lay of the land do you need to see to get to a place you haven't been?* Farn answered in a way he hope his man would understand, *I do not*

need to see how to get there, I need to see where to go and I will go there.
Kaxil humphed and sighed as he eyed Akail. "Akail, have you
ever tried to speak to a dragon?" Akail looked up in wonder.
"No sir. It is forbidden of slaves to do so." Kaxil nodded, "I
know, but if you could show Farn a memory of your home, or
the land around it…." Akail stood and finished the sentence,
"He could bring us home!" Akail glanced over at the dragon
whose great horned head was raised and gazing intently at him.
Kaxil walked over to Farn, *Farn, please try to hear the boy.* Farn
sounded almost offended as he replied, *If I want to hear him, I shall
hear him.* Kaxil chuckled, "Alright Akail just try to show Farn
what you remember. Akail walked up slowly to Farn. He didn't
know why but he put out his hand and Kaxil was amazed to see
Farn reach out his nose and accept the touch. Akail closed his
eyes and thought of home.

Later that day Farn was flying the two young men over green
countryside. Soon they were within sight of the sea and Akail
thumped Kaxil's arm and pointed out to the sea. Both sat
dumbfounded as they gazed out upon the vast blueness. Akail
saw now with his eyes what his heart and body had experienced.
Freedom. A bond had been severed, what had been kept from
view for so long was now revealed and he sang out with a shout
of joyful exuberance. He suddenly could not wait to see his
home before him as he now saw the waves, un barred by the
dark walls of the Keep that had for so many years been his
prison.

Kaxil's eyes were scanning the other horizon and noticed
not far away, a pillar of smoke rising in the distance. Kaxil
questioned Farn, *What's happened there?* Farn replied, *Where we go*

is burning. Kaxil's thoughts seemed to scramble in his head. *Farn! Don't go straight there, swing back and land in the woods to the east, fly low and out of sight.* Kaxil looked around feeling suddenly stupid and helpless. He thought of Akail, how could he save him from death only to deliver him to grief! Stupid! Kaxil realized the Keep had only needed to find the dragon who had collected Akail eight years ago, that's what he would have done. As they landed Akail wanted answers but Kaxil could give him none. He needed to know what was going on. *Farn, can you tell what's burning?* Farn raised his nose and sniffed the air as they dismounted. They were less than two miles from the site and Kaxil turned his face toward the cloud of smoke his eyes burning like embers of fire. Farn answered after a moment, *wood, a house I think.* Kaxil pressured him, *What about flesh?* Farn answered softly, *No, I smell no death.* The rider asked, *what about dragons?* Farn sighed, *I cannot hear them, but there is a faint smell, I am not certain.* Kaxil made up his mind. Akail was watching the rider intently waiting to know what was going on. Kaxil turned toward him, "Akail, Farn says that smoke is coming from your home." Akail looked to the sky and grew anxious. Kaxil continued, "We're going to approach on foot. These woods should cover us until we're close enough to see what's going on."

They approached a clearing in a small meadow surrounded by woods. Within the clearing, the remnants of a small house smoldered and smoked. Akail darted past Kaxil, unaware of any danger, toward his home. He stopped just short of the smoking heap and crumpled to his knees with great sobs. Kaxil wasn't far behind him, "Akail! Akail, I'm sorry! I should have told you," he then was caught up to the boy, "Akail, Farn says he smells no death! No one was in there." Akail looked up at him with waves of relief washing over his face. He stood up and wiped his face. And then began to look around, but before they could look for anyone, a dragon's blaze lashed around them from above. The flames only just missed them as a shriek was heard in the air above them. Falling to the ground with Akail under him, Kaxil turned to see Farn bringing down Galot and Fabir. The two dragons crumpled to the ground and tumbled apart. Farn was up first and roared a challenge to the large silver dragon, but the other did not move. His great neck had been broken when he fell. Farn approached his fallen brother slowly and cautiously. The rider lay a few feet from his dragon's body. Kaxil approached the rider with his sword drawn. Akail sidestepped away yet watched carefully as Kaxil extended his sword out to flip the man over. Fabir's body moved limply at first but before his back hit the ground he jumped up and their swords met in the air. Kaxil stepped back and swung his blade wide forcing the other man to step back as well. They moved slowly at first, stepping in a circular pattern eyeing each other warily. Kaxil wondered what Fabir's orders were and if there were any other dragon's nearby. Farn answered his thoughts; *Galot did not have time to call them.* Kaxil spoke, "You're all alone, Fabir, drop your sword and I'll let you walk out of here." Fabir was struggling already from the loss of his dragon. He appeared to nearly double over, as he was racked with inner pain and loss. His mind felt lonely and sorrow shattered his thoughts. Yet his blood was pumping with rage, and he forced himself upright. "You've turned on your own, Kaxil! What are you going to do? Turn your dragon into a plow horse and live among the simpletons? I have a hard time picturing it!" Kaxil was ready but unwilling to strike first, "Just leave Fabir. I have no wish to hurt you." Fabir's eyes burned and he lunged, Kaxil could do nothing but his best work against such passionate rage. Kaxil seemed to go into battle mode and his blade appeared like a glinting glass in the sun. Fabir was unarmed quickly and Kaxil stood toward him with his sword point extended, keeping Fabir back. The other rider turned and gazed at his fallen dragon. Although his eyes saw the dragon, his mind was empty there was no longer anything there, no presence, no faithful words, only darkness. Fabir turned back, hunched over, his eyes desperate for help. He looked to Kaxil, his enemy, yet still a rider. Fabir spoke, "I can't walk away." Yet his eyes asked Kaxil for release. Escape from the half-existence of a dragonless rider. Kaxil stood unmoving, he knew what was coming and his eyes were heavy with the weight of it. Fabir screamed and lunged himself toward Kaxil's sword. Fabir was surprised as Kaxil side stepped and brought the bit of his sword across the back of his head. Then he fell into a lonely darkness.

Kaxil gently set his body to rest on the soft grass. Kaxil and Farn sat motionless under the weight of the tragedy before them. Akail stood beside his master, "There's no going back for you now is there?" Kaxil kept his eyes on Fabir's face as he answered, "There never was." He then turned toward Farn. *Friend, please take him just outside of the nearest town and leave him there.* Farn came and gently picked up the unconscious man and flew off. Kaxil watched Farn in the sky and looked around. They would not be safe here for long, yet he wanted Akail to have some time here, and he needed some time to consider where they would go from here. It wouldn't be easy to hide a dragon. Kaxil's thoughts were heavy, what kind of life was there before him now?

Later, it was Kaxil who found an old grave site and spoke to Akail. Apparently his father had died sometime prior. Akail stood numbly looking at the grave marker. Kaxil glanced up at the sky. There was still no trace of Akail's mother. Kaxil doubted greatly that they would have taken her alive. He watched Akail as the wind began to beat against his thin frame. Akail shivered as his body cooled and began to feel as raw and achy as his heart.

Kaxil awoke in the crook of Farn's arm to a crash and a bang, whose sound was diminished by a distance. Farn grumbled and spoke to his rider without lifting an eyelid. *The boy is looking for something.* Kaxil got up and followed the ruckus. They had camped across the glen in the woods, well away from the homestead. Akail had obviously awakened early and headed back, Kaxil meandered in the general direction. *Farn, keep your ears open will you?* He looked around. A great pity welled up within him and he set his jaw as he gave a heavy sigh. They needed to get away from here, the sooner the better. It was only a matter of time before the Keep sent another dragon or two.

More crashing, boards slapped together, something was thrown and broken. Kaxil strode quickly over to his page, "Akail." The young man ignored his master's approach. Kaxil called to him again, "Akail." But he only grew more violent in the urgency of his search. Kaxil grabbed him and shook him. Akail struggled, "Let go!" The youth shouted in anger, frustration, and pain. Kaxil held him firm and spoke, "You won't find it. You can't get it back, nothing will bring it back!" He spoke firmly, knowing the words were harsh but necessary. Akail wriggled fiercely out of Kaxil's grasp, "What would you know?!" He shouted at the rider as he shoved him in the chest. Kaxil stood silently, strong and unmoving like the truth Akail hated to acknowledge. The comfort of a home he only remembered was now lost forever. Akail fell to his knees and wept, Kaxil was right. He would never find what he was truly looking for; the lost years of his childhood. Kaxil turned and stepped out into the grass yard. He wasn't sure how to help. Everything Kaxil was feeling now was contrary to the way he had thought and felt about others before. Pity, regret, compassion for the Sea Folk filled him and he longed for release. He looked to the sky and within him his heart threw out a great battle cry as he felt an overwhelming desire to do right by these simple people. In the hills behind them, a dragon bugled as Farm vocalized what he felt from his rider. Kaxil looked around feeling lost. His eyes fell to a small leather pouch, which lay in the grass.

Akail's heart was calling, out to someone or something to let him know that he was not utterly alone. Could his mother be alive, he doubted it. His family had been his hope, his dream. The thought that he would be with them again, that he might know joy and laughter with them again had gotten him through so much within the dark hollows of stone where he had been prisoner. His heart wavered: what he had dreamt of in freedom was gone. Only a truth he had been unprepared for was set before him. An empty hollow loneliness threatened to consume him.

The wind blew around him, stirring his hair and his heart. *You are never alone.* Light shone upon his heart and a warm strength filled him. *Your grief will pass, but I have a hope and a future for you.* Akail blinked as he pondered the idea rather than wondering where it had come from. *I am your mother, I am your father, and I have sent you a brother, so you will not be alone.* Akail understood and looked up to see Kaxil picking something up out of the grass. *You were taken from your home, and have now lost a family you loved. He has left his home, to find a family he never knew he had.* Akail wondered at the words, but felt comforted and lifted his eyes to the sky. He had been heard and answered. As he stood, Kaxil walked back toward him. "Akail, look at this." Kaxil held out the pouch and the stone he had found within it. Akail smiled through his tears as he grabbed it from Kaxil's hand. "This is hers! Kaxil, this is my mothers. She always wore it around her neck. Look, look! The string isn't broken! She had to have taken it off, she left it." He burst out in a fresh wave of tears. Kaxil stood stupidly as his slave clasped onto him. And suddenly he realized that he cared for Akail. This child he had practically raised, this young man who had served him so well, felt his master's arms around him in a brotherly embrace.

Kaxil and Akail walked back through the woods toward Farn. Kaxil swung up on his dragon. Akail looked up and asked, "Do we have any idea where we are going?" Kaxil actually laughed, "Yes, we're going to follow the light."

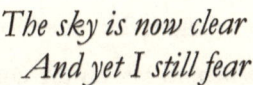

The sky is now clear
And yet I still fear

The water still speaks
My heart feels so weak

The words were so clear
The message so near

I will hope, I will wait
What now is my fate?

25

Aylia looked up as a dragon flew overhead. She shivered at the sight of it. Looking behind her up the coastline she saw Japha and Oya. A sweet smile swept her face. Turning around she left the sandy floor and began to climb up the rocky mountain terrain. She soon found a boulder to her liking and sat in the shadow of the trees gazing at the Sea. The watery layer of her eyes reflected the picturesque horizon before her. The wind blew and the leaves and piney bows of the trees fluttered around her. So much had happened in such a short time. Aylia looked back toward Japha and Oya. She wondered about their homes and how long they would wait until any of them would be able to get words to their families or start to travel home.

The intense pain and tragedy of what had happened to Barduuk was ebbing away. Hope was being stirred. The water before her was vast and the distant horizon seemed full of unknown potential. Lifting her eyes again to the open sea her thoughts turned back to the rumors. Sitting up, away from the water, where she could not hear the words, she let herself doubt. She had heard the stories, many had come and sat at Fahim's table and spoken of Barduuk, of strange tales of seeing him, back from the dead. And Aylia believed them. She still remembered some of the first phrases the water had spoken about him, *"he comes, he goes, he ebbs, he flows.* She sat pondering the words, and the roar of triumph she now heard in the distance waves. She wondered what was really possible, and what was on the other side of this great body of water.

The wind gusted and Aylia glanced up, expecting to see another dragon winging over her. A large form hovered directly overhead, blocking out the sun. Aylia had to shut her eyes as it moved and unveiled the light. Standing up Aylia felt a bit unnerved as it landed behind her. She watched the silhouette of a man as he dismounted the large figure. She did not want to be so near to a dragon. She was headed down the hill toward her friends when she heard her name, *"Aylia."* Her small frame stopped in her tracks.

The sound, the voice was so familiar. As if she had heard it in a dream. When she turned around she was able to see the man standing near the head of a large winged creature; that was definitely *not* a dragon. She was able to see only dark silhouette's encased in rays of light. The man turned and stepped away before Aylia got a good look at his face. Aylia's feet were frozen in their spot as large white hand like paws padded along the ground toward her. The light changed and Aylia was able to see it clearly. Here in front of her was the strange white winged animal she had seen in her dreams. It stopped moving nearly twenty feet from her and stared at the slight figure of a girl with large black eyes. Aylia took in every feature. It was beautiful. Setting itself down on its haunches and letting its wings down slightly it called to Aylia again. *"Hello, little one."* Aylia couldn't speak. She didn't even know what she would have said.

The beast was covered in soft white fur and gave itself and slight shake and raised a paw to its long nose to get at an itch. It then sat still and stately and with a gentle bow if its head. Before Aylia was aware of a thought or question within herself she heard an answer, *"I am the Beginning."* The voice was deep but feminine and resonated through Aylia's head and heart, not her ears. The Beginning, Aylia wondered, of what? A soft purring chuckle filled Aylia's soul. *"I am not a beginning, but The Beginning. I am the Origin, the Wellspring from which all things begin.* The Beginning nodded and let her eyelids fall and rise again slowly. *"He is here, loved one."* Aylia shook her head and would have run from the spot had she not been caught by the presence of the man that stepped forward from behind the Beginning's wing. Aylia looked him over carefully. He wore strange clothing; his hair and skin were pure white and his eyes dark and loving. He spoke and a joy bubbled within Aylia's chest at the sound, "Well, hello Aylia. It is good to see you again." Aylia blinked and looked again. His features seemed uncertain, as if they faltered for a moment and she saw Barduuk's face superimposed over this one. She knew that this was he, but she couldn't wrap her head around just how that was possible. He laughed. "Do I look different to you?" Aylia nodded very slowly. He continued, "Well that is to be expected. I should look different; I am not as I was." He leaned down toward her a bit and winked as he said, "Death can do that to a person." She opened her mouth to speak but nothing came out and she smiled as she was overcome by the peace of his presence. He stood up and looked past her toward Japha and Oya, who were below in the sand.

Turning back to Aylia he spoke, "It is me, Aylia. I want you to know that things are not always as they seem, not even death. Do you understand?" Aylia tried to nod, but couldn't force a polite, yet false answer and ended up shaking her head. He laughed as her honest response. "You will, in time, little sister." His eyes glinted with joy, and Aylia was affronted by the remorse in her heart. "I am sorry." The words were soft and she barely remembered saying them. He knelt down hear her and took her hand. The motion was as it had been when they had met, only this time it was not raining, and no water filled her hand. He smiled as he touched the palm of her hand. More beauty and love than she could ever hope to comprehend flooded her, and she saw grace and absolute love.

The moment passed away almost as quickly as it had overtaken her and she smiled through her tears as she and her savior shared a look of perfect understanding. He then tilted his head toward the Beginning, "Wanna take her out for a spin?" Aylia looked up at the great white wings and back at Barduuk in disbelief. She couldn't find her voice. Barduuk threw his head back and laughed again. "It's time for you to see some things." He spoke decisively. Without waiting for her to find her voice he took hold of Aylia and threw her up onto the Beginning. She was barely able to grab on before they were in the air with on great leap off of the small cliff she had been sitting on. The wind blew her hair from her face and she began to laugh despite the sudden change.

The Beginning beat her wings and took them high into the sky. They parted small wisps of clouds and Aylia heard the tiny water vapors gasp in amused astonishment as they were abased in such a way. Aylia giggled at them. She leaned forward and buried her face in the thick white fur, discovering that the Beginning smelt lovely, like fresh flowers and a deep penetrating type of spice. Gold dust fluttered out of her fur and clung to Aylia's eyelashes and hair. They flew higher until Aylia could begin to see the stars glinting through the fading blueness of sky.

Aylia looked down and saw the sea. They were far from the shore now, and the water looked calm and reflected fully the sky and clouds. Aylia was caught by the reflection it actually appeared as if they were flying over, looking down on the sky, not a sea. Aylia lifted her eyes and looked back up and saw rolling waves above her, for the sky was rolling like the water. Weightlessness consumed Aylia and she nearly floated off of the

Beginnings neck. *Don't let go now, we're almost there!* The Beginnings call gave her strength and she gripped the long white hairs. The flying creature flipped suddenly in the air and Aylia was shaken as the weightlessness passed. Aylia watched the turbulent sky beneath them. Although it moved like water Aylia was amazed to see that it was still the sky and what looked like breaking waves were bands of light that seemed to splash and dance upon the edges of the universe. She watched them until they cascaded upon an unfamiliar shore.

A great country rose out of the depths of the living sky. Mountains made of gems, rivers that flowed with light, and other living things that moved and flickered just out of her sight. The Beginning landed just past the surf and Aylia slid off. Caught in the atmosphere of the place Aylia hugged the Beginning and laughed. The sky appeared like night, yet it was light as day, for the land itself shone in every hue of color. Aylia loved the way the Beginning seemed to change color as she was caressed by different rays of light.

Aylia was gazing to the mountains and the light beyond when the Beginning called her back. *Aylia, you are here to see the sand of this shore.* They walked down a long stretch of the shore and Aylia looked at the sand, it wasn't like sand on her home at all. Aylia bent down and scooped up a handful of it and saw that it was very small pearl like grains. She turned to the Beginning, and the Beginning was chuckling. *They are pearls. For every one of you who are called from that shore, a place, a reservation is made here, as a pearl.* Aylia's hand suddenly felt heavy as if the value of the sand in her hand had given it a great weight. She set the pearls down gently and was amazed when the Beginning sat and began digging with great sweeps of her hand like paws into the shore. *Help me Aylia. We are to dig for an oyster.* Aylia came near and began to dig. The Beginning reprimanded her, *No, you dig with your feet.*

Aylia stood and moved her toes through the sand and soon found that there was much water just beneath the surface. A boggy muddy feeling crept up her legs as she seemed to sink into the shore. She lifted her legs, one at a time bringing up to the surface, what had been unseen a moment before. A wind began to blow and the waves of the sea tossed and light flashed in the sea and sky light living lightening. Aylia looked up from her work to the heavenly storm, but was called back by the Beginning. *There isn't much time, keep digging.* Only one at first, and then two, sometimes three, Aylia began to pull the strange mollusks from the sand. Then as suddenly as it had started, the wind died down and a great light fell on them.

The sea flooded over with the color blue and Aylia looked out over the water; then around her twirled shimmering wings of a type of little butterfly. *They are not butterflies, Aylia. These are our oysters.* Aylia lifted a hand as if to touch one but the wings fluttered away from her grasp and a tiny figure was revealed. Aylia gasped as she saw what appeared like a tiny woman with wings. She then realized that the wings were the delicate type of shells of the oysters and when she had brought them to the surface they must have awakened. The tiny person wore lovely raiment and smiled at Aylia. "I never imagined that oysters might be like this on the Other Shore." The Beginning looked out across the cosmic sea before them. *They were once much like this on your shore Aylia.* Aylia turned puzzled by this remark. The Beginning continued, *You understand the world around you by what you see and know Aylia, but I was there when it began and I remember your home as it was in me.* The Beginning held a silence for a long time and Aylia could feel a beautiful type of sorrow. Finally the Beginning continued, *The world was made full of light that gave it life as it is here. Yet now that light has been diminished, it is like a green jungle that has now become a desert. Now the King places a piece of dirt in a tiny creature on your shore, and over time reveals the mystery of redemption. By the making of a pearl he shows you how he hopes to restore what is to what he once made it to be. That is why your reservation is held by a pearl, for He will turn what you are, a speck of dust, into what you are destined to be, a living pearl.* Aylia stepped close and placed a hand on the large white neck. *He went to your shore, to redeem you Aylia. Look at this sand made of pearls and know that you are one of many that are loved by the King.*

Aylia strode toward the water. The dazzling beauty of the place was beyond description. It penetrated her very being. She didn't just feel the colors and lights that danced around her in this place, she could feel them and taste them and hear them all at once.

Aylia watched the strange looking water and wondered about the water words. "Was it the King that spoke to me through the water?" The Beginning answered her, *Yes Aylia. Water can be a messenger. The King needed you to be prepared for the journey before you, so he sent you messages in the water. And as your faith grew, light shone in your spirit and began to awaken the water. The water also brought you the very sound of his voice. Water, Fire, Wind, even the Earth all have the ability to carry what you call words, from this shore. They are the ancient doors that were established in my youth. They are not without consciousness, man has simply fallen from the office of their steward and interpreter as you were destined to be. They are now bound to action or stillness more than speech. Yet, when the essence of the Maker, which is Light, shines on the elements, they will awaken and their voices will be heard by men again. Barduuk came to be the first doorway of this Light onto your shore, to show you what you are to be. You are to be living pearls, glowing spirits that give light into the dark room that is your home. You are to open, as the King bids you, these ancient doors. Aylia, you heard the water speak, because you heart shone with the Light of your faith in the King, and the water was affected by it. The Light that dwells within your heart shone onto the water, and the water was revived ever so much. The water needs light in order to speak, just as you need air. When men chose darkness, the King left your shores so long ago His light went with him and the world grew dim. The elemental and creaturely entities lost their voices and were reduced to moans and groaning. They have been waiting for the sons and daughters of the Light to come forth. They have been waiting for such as you are called to be."* Aylia looked down and touched her chest, she thought of the deep pounding and warmth she felt there at times. Aylia looked up at her fluffy friend, "And what of the voice of the Deep?" The large white head bobbed as she walked and her eyes smiled at the thought of the deep, *"Don't forget that water not only reflects light, but also allows it to pass through it. The voice of the deep is the voice of the Father of Lights. His messages are heavy and can only be held in the depths. He speaks on this shore in eternity, future, past and present, all at once, realized in one, but on your world it must wash upon the sands of time, one wave after another. His voice is in the water, for the water has the capacity to remember Him."*

Look at the Sea Aylia. There is no longer a Veil to hinder you from seeing this shore, but there are still miles upon miles of separation. You will find the same separation in your heart and the hearts of others when it comes to accepting the truth. Remember, water may have brought you his words, but water does not travel on its own strength, it is moved by the pull of the earth and the breath of the wind. So will you, not need to carry what He's placed in you by your own strength, but simply let the words rest in you; just as the water let's words rest in it. And you will speak, either when the King pushes you with the presence of the light, or the need of others causes you to speak in love."

The Beginning reared up on her hindquarters and spread her wings as she let out a call of victory. The cry caused the sea to roll away from the shore. The ripples tumbled and ran like a herd of dear spooked by a lion. Aylia looked up and laughed. The Beginning lowered herself down and spoke again to Aylia. *"Be watchful, daughter, are about to see many happenings as I move. For every beginning I am to make, I must also be an end to something else.*

They took another path home and were once again on the sandy shore of men. Coming down the beach Aylia could see Japha and Oya's silhouettes as they spoke to a third person. She turned toward the Beginning and asked, "Will *He* remain with us for long?" The Beginning looked up the shoreline then turned her head toward, *"No,"* she said shaking her great head, *"Soon, I will carry him to his Father. But I will return"*, the Beginning moved her large head close to Aylia so the girl could see the depth of her eye. Within the dark sphere Aylia trembled as she saw a dance of light and color as sparks flickered within as the Beginning spoke of what was to come, *"and I will not be alone when I do."*

Aylia was shown many things that day, and in days after, she visited the other shore whenever she was called, while awake or dreaming. On her own shore she could never fully remember all of the things from the Other, but enough remained. On that day, as she stood with the Beginning, she heard the water sing:

"We know, we show, we ebb, we flow.
The Prince shall go, the King shall know,
When He shall send a holy flight,
And fill this shore with shadows bright."

The End

About the Author

JESSICA HECKET was born in Coeur d'Alene, Idaho, and has grown up in the surrounding areas. She met God when she was seven years old and has loved him ever since. She is now a wife and mother whose art and dreams are often inspired by God and infused with her love of nature and horses.

www.ingramcontent.com/pod-product-compliance
Lightning Source LLC
Chambersburg PA
CBHW031246120726
47905CB00002B/745